THE GARDEN OF
EARTHLY DELIGHTS

THE GARDEN OF EARTHLY DELIGHTS

JACK'S STORY

GORDON YATES

authorHOUSE®

AuthorHouse™
1663 Liberty Drive
Bloomington, IN 47403
www.authorhouse.com
Phone: 1-800-839-8640

First published by AuthorHouse   10/04/2011

ISBN: 978-1-4567-9725-6 (sc)

Printed in the United States of America

CHAPTER 1

THE FINE RAIN had settled on top of Jack's thick, dark, mop of hair. He hardly noticed as rivulets ran down his cheeks and neck until they stained the collar of his grey, school shirt. He was preoccupied with far more important problems. With a resigned sigh he inserted his MP3 Player earphones and adjusted the volume.

The leaden sky, reflected in the rain soaked pavement of the north London street, intensified his melancholic mood. A lone rook wheeled lazily overhead, its raucous call echoing eerily from the low clouds, as though mocking his dissatisfaction. He gazed at the steady stream of morning traffic nudging through the drizzle, and shivered, the cold and damp finally penetrating his unsuitable clothing. His future seemed destined to be dull and boring, like the smug middle class houses on each side of the street.

His mind drifted back to the worrying statement made by his father, at breakfast earlier: "You should quickly become a fully fledged solicitor", he had said with undisguised excitement. He had been leading up to this for some time, and Jack had been dreading it. Nigel Dawkins had obviously pulled strings in the firm and arranged for his only child's future. Once he had decided, he would accept no argument. It had always been that way.

Jack would be required to study law at university, graduate with a good degree, enter his father's firm and settle down to a safe and self satisfied life. The prospect filled him with dread.

He did not wish to be disloyal, but it was, after all, *his* future which was being decided for him. He would have to make a stand sometime and that time was rapidly approaching. His 'A' level choices had already disrupted his father's plans; science subjects were not going to contribute to a career as a solicitor. Undaunted, his father had pointed out that he need not have a degree in law to qualify. It simply meant a detour onto something he had called a "Common Professional Examination", or "Graduate Diploma in Law", before he would complete the "Legal Practice Course". At that point Jack had switched off, perceiving that to be the least controversial thing to do. Now the turmoil in his mind was compounded by the uneasy sensation that there was something different, something unreal, about this morning. It was as though someone was peering over his shoulder, a stranger rummaging intrusively in his private thoughts.

He kicked at a loose stone. Startled, he watched as it bounded along the pavement for an alarming distance, stopped, and then proceeded to roll again finally coming to rest at the feet of another, much younger, tormentor. The stone's strange behaviour was forgotten and he groaned inwardly as he saw her. His morning had been terrible so far and now this!

He hitched his book bag higher on his prematurely broad shoulders and continued on his way to school, determinedly trying to ignore and avoid Megan Carter. She quickly caught up with him.

'So! Throwing bricks now is it?' she demanded.

Her tall, slim athletic figure, toned by gymnastic training, was widely admired by the male population of the school and envied by the female. She seemed oblivious to the affect she had on either sex, her air of innocence serving to make her more appealing.

Jack's mother had decided that Megan was just the sort of girl she would like as a daughter-in-law and it was obvious to everyone at school, except Jack, that Megan agreed with her. He did not dislike her but she represented the very lifestyle he wished to avoid. The last thing he needed this morning was her banal chatter when he was trying to assemble some coherent thoughts around his future.

Her large, heavily lidded, hazel eyes rested on him momentarily, critically noting his carelessly dressed appearance. The crumpled trousers resting on his scuffed black shoes, his tie, pencil thin with the knot halfway down his unbuttoned shirt and all covered in a fine mist of rain. He flinched, waiting for the expected onslaught.

'Trying to avoid me, were you? And you dressed like that! Look at you,' she said, flicking his tie with her finger. 'You look as though you've just been sicked up by a cat.' She tilted her head backwards and looked down her small nose at him for emphasis.

He side stepped the finger jabbing at his chest, shrugged his shoulders dismissively, and made to walk on, whereupon Megan quickly confronted him once more.

'You can't avoid the inevitable boyo,' she said, smiling up at him, 'you are a marked man!'

'Whatever!' he grunted.

They walked along together and she continued a one-sided conversation in her husky voice about other teenage relationships within the school as Jack turned up the volume of his MP3 Player. He glanced sideways and watched her mouth moving for a few seconds, convinced that nothing of any importance was coming out of those full red lips.

Then, suddenly he stopped and, listening intently, pressed on his earphones. Megan continued for a few paces, realised he had stopped and turned to remonstrate with him.

'What?' she cried, 'What is it?'

'Nothing, you go on!'

She noticed his face was animated with disbelief. They carried on for a few yards and Jack paused again.

Megan was irritated, 'I do wish you wouldn't listen to that thing while I'm trying to talk to you.' She leaned towards his ear, 'You know it's rude to listen to that while someone is trying to talk to you,' she repeated emphatically.

'Don't you mean talk at?' he said under his breath. He waved her away and snapped, 'Shush! I'm trying to listen to something important.'

Megan, startled at this uncharacteristic outburst, stepped back off the pavement, her foot splashing in a puddle. 'Oh and I suppose I'm not important?' she cried haughtily, shaking her soggy foot.

Jack didn't respond, he was completely absorbed, frozen in a statue like pose on the pavement. She aimed a kick at his ankle, turned sharply then with a purposeful stride continued walking on her own muttering, 'Ignorant little schoolboy so he is, I really don't know what I see in him.'

Intrigued, she glanced back at him after a short while. He was still motionless, concentrating on something as though his life depended on it. She shrugged, set her face in determined fashion against the drizzle and continued on her way to school.

Finally with a frown, Jack slowly began to place one foot in front of another and hesitatingly followed her.

Greystone Grammar School was aptly named, having an impressive solid frontage blackened over time by the ravages of sulphur laden London smog. Jack looked up at the familiar cloisters and sighed. There was no sign of Megan, who, irritated by Jack's unusual behaviour, had disappeared inside and hurried off to the first lesson of the day.

Mr. Smith's 'A' level Physics class was not renowned for holding the attention of its pupils. He was quite used to being confronted with thirty vacant expressions this early in the morning so Jack's attracted no special attention. His mind was still occupied with the behaviour of his MP3 Player. What he had heard didn't seem possible, but he was certain it had happened and he hadn't dreamed it.

Megan was seated at the desk in front of him, her blond ponytail flicking as she moved her head this way and that. She turned around, smiled, and smacked his hand with her ruler. There was a grunt from the front of the classroom as Smithy noticed the minor disturbance. Jack studiously ignored her, his eyes glazed and distant.

The voice had been urgent, appealing, and had called him by name, 'Jack! Help me!' she had said. *It was a strange accent*, he thought*, sort of lilting*, *a bit like Megan's Welsh accent*. He reckoned Megan only put that on for effect as, although her mother came from Wales, she had never lived there.

Of course it could just have been a coincidence; a radio station possibly, breaking through in his earphones broadcasting a play with someone in it called Jack. He pondered on this possibility for a while. Finally, convincing himself that it was the only sensible explanation, he decided to give it no more thought.

Megan turned back to face Smithy, propped her chin on cupped hands and gazed at him as he droned on about atomic energy levels. She reflected on Jack's offhand behaviour. His reluctance to return her previous amorous advances did not prevent her imagination conjuring up visions of an intimate relationship. Her little finger strayed to her lips and, barely touching them began gently to caress their sensitive surface. She could almost feel Jack's lips brush her cheek and shuddered with pleasure.

Jack had his faults, she was well aware of that. He tended to be indecisive and unsure of himself. That could change with time and a little help from her. His physique was second to none and he was handsome, in a Mediterranean sort of way. Gradually her reverie was dispelled as her eyes involuntarily focussed on Smithy whose enquiring gaze was directly upon her.

He was a wiry bony little man whose spectacles constantly teetered on the tip of his beak like, nose. Shrouded in overgrown eyebrows, his eyes were barely visible between the top of his spectacles and the unlikely growth descending on them from above. Hair on his shiny, billiard-ball head was sparse in contrast.

Rumours about Smithy were various and lurid, completely at odds with his desiccated appearance. All manner of theories had developed around the late middle-aged, unspectacular, unmarried recluse but none had ever been proven. He was as much a mystery to this particular sixth form as those of three decades ago. One thing was undeniably true; his teaching method remained unaltered from the day he had graduated. It consisted of reading from the scrawl filling several ancient, tatty, exercise books which he had preserved from his own days in the sixth form in the very classroom where he now taught.

A moment of panic seized her as she realised that if Jack pursued a career in teaching, he could become as dry and withered as Smithy. She decided that must not be allowed to happen. He must have an interesting, exciting and glamorous lifestyle. She visualised herself as the wife of a premiership footballer, after all, Jack was captain of the very successful school football team and who knows where that may lead? Having satisfied herself on that score, she returned to the business of his strange behaviour on the way to school. Recalling how he had stopped suddenly while listening to his MP3 Player and the incredulous expression on his face, she resolved to follow him out of school that evening and challenge him about it.

The pencil between Jack's fingers began to squirm. Startled, he dropped it with a clatter on the desk, whereupon it propelled itself across the classroom and landed neatly in Smithy's ancient inkpot.

Mr. Smith peered over his glasses at him, 'Not the place to practice your Beckham free kicks Dawkins,' he intoned waspishly, fishing the offending pencil out.

Jack blushed and went to rescue it, to the accompaniment of much suppressed mirth from the rest of the class. 'Sorry sir; accident, I didn't mean to . . . ,' he stuttered.

He resumed his seat and turned the pencil over in his fingers, holding onto it very tightly. In astonishment he noticed the normal gold lettering along its length had been transformed. It now read, "Jack you must help me!" He stared at it in disbelief, what was going on? Glancing around at his classmates, he hastily stuffed it into his pocket.

After that incident concentration was impossible. The feeling of being scrutinised intensified as the day wore on until Jack was anxiously fidgeting in lectures, concerned about what may happen next. Nothing did, so with relief and earphones in place he finally strode out of school that evening, unaware that Megan was carefully following a few paces behind.

Although there had been no further strange incidents during the day, there had been a dramatic change in his attitude to his career decision. For some reason he could not understand, the conflict raging in the Dawkins household no longer seemed important. Having decided to confront his father over the matter, he felt in control of his own life, for better . . . or worse! So where had this sudden burst of courage come from?

The MP3 Player began to crackle and he remembered that this had preceded the strange voice he had heard earlier. He stopped walking and pressed the earphones hard into his ears straining to hear something.

'JACK!'

It was so loud that he instinctively pulled the earphones out then desperately scrambled to stuff them back in again. His abrupt stop had caused Megan to stumble into him from behind. A crowd of giggling schoolgirls enabled her to remain inconspicuous as she merged in with them. He was totally absorbed and would not have noticed her anyway.

'Don't shout!' he protested, and was staggered to hear the reply,

'OK! Listen carefully.'

'H . . . h . . . how can you hear me?'

'Never mind that, you have to do something for me.'

Megan's curiosity, aroused by his unusual antics, could no longer be contained, and she confronted him; 'Started talking to yourself now is it? Come on, it's spooky around here,' she said, pulling on his arm.

'What do you mean?' he said, momentarily distracted from the voice in his earphones.

She inclined her head in the direction of an insignificant house directly in front of them, 'It's haunted,' she said simply.

'You don't believe that garbage do you?'

She leaned closer to him and with a knowing wink whispered, 'Strange lights at the dead of night, weird unearthly sounds . . . ,'she rolled her eyes for emphasis.

'You're just trying to wind me up,' cut in Jack impatiently.

'What's so interesting in here then?' she exclaimed, making a grab for the earphones.

The voice shouted, 'Get rid of her!' as he dodged her flailing arm.

'Sod off! Can't you see I'm trying to listen to something?'

This time she was not to be deflected, ignoring the expletive, which for him was unusual, she grabbed one of the earphones and pushed it into her ear. The other fell from his ear and trailed on the ground. The triumphant expression on her face quickly changed to displeasure and then anguish. She tore out the earphone, threw it at Jack and with tears in her eyes ran down the street, pausing only to shout over her shoulder, 'I hate you! I'll never speak to you again Jack Dawkins. You're disgusting, listening to filthy stuff like that!'

'Phew!' he said, 'I wonder what all that was about.' Refitting the earphones in his ears he addressed the voice, 'What did you say to her?'

'Never mind, you wouldn't understand. Now Jack, you have to help me.'

'I do? But . . . .'

'Don't move! Stay where you are!'

He froze and looking furtively around whispered, 'Why?'

'You see that house directly in front of you?'

'Yes, you mean the one Megan said was haunted?'

'Silly girl, of course it's not haunted. I want you to get into it.'

The house in question was an unremarkable detached town house with a small front garden, a low brick wall at the front and the number fourteen in brass numerals on the front door. The upstairs front room curtains were closed, otherwise there was no outward sign of habitation. Megan's warning echoed in his head, "it's haunted", she had said. He felt his spine tingle, as though an icicle had been dragged up it. He shuddered. Thinking the voice had gone, he began to move off.

'Jack! I'm desperate, please help me!'

He felt his irritation and curiosity growing in equal measure. 'I don't break into other peoples houses,' he said, wishing he could bring an end to the bizarre conversation.

There was a pause; he looked around to confirm he was not being watched. The street had emptied of students by now, so feeling more confident he decided to try and understand what was going on, 'How do you know my name, how are you talking to me . . . who are you?'

She cut him short, 'I'll explain all that once you get me out of this mess.'

'What mess? Why do you want me to break into somebody's house, are you a burglar?'

'It's not *somebody's* house, it's mine!'

'You're locked out? Where are you?'

He turned around swiftly, half expecting to see the owner of the voice peering over his shoulder. No one was there.

'Just do as I say and stop behaving like an idiot,' snapped the voice testily.

He looked up and down the street and although it was already dark, could just make out in the street lights the shape of an enormous hairy man approaching in the distance.

'Oh no!' he whispered to himself, 'Megan's father!'

Fortunately, he had not been seen, so fearing a confrontation he slipped into the garden of the house and quickly made his way round to the back. He crouched down by a large conservatory, which ran almost the full length of the building. A high privet hedge screened the garden from neighbours to the rear.

The palms of his hands were beginning to sweat and his knees were trembling uncontrollably. *Why am I getting myself into this?* he thought.

'Because you're a knight in shining armour and I am definitely a damsel in distress,' said the voice with a low chuckle.

Although it was a cold evening in November, Jack could feel the sweat break out on his forehead as fear gripped and squeezed his stomach into a tight little knot.

'H . . . h . . . how did you know what I was thinking?' he stammered.

'Sorry Jack, I didn't mean to frighten you but this is a matter of life and death, please do as I ask.'

'Why can't I just knock on the door?' he inquired and immediately regretted saying it. *Haunted house! Knock on the door! What am I thinking of?*

'I'm beginning to wish I'd picked someone else,' retorted the voice curtly.

'Picked?' cried Jack, in alarm, 'What do you mean by that?'

The voice ignored him, 'The conservatory key is under the water butt at the bottom of the garden,' she said.

This positive response jerked him into action. *Well I don't suppose letting myself into someone's house with their permission is a crime,* he thought, *and she does know the location of the key. But, why can't she get it for herself?*

Sure enough it was where she had said it would be. This gave him confidence to continue. He turned and looked back at the house which was presenting a dark outline against the orange glare of street lamps. He glanced at his watch, half past four; he might just make it home in time for tea without arousing suspicion. As though sensing his indecision the voice cut into his thoughts.

'Please get on with it.'

He padded across the lawn, slipped the key into the lock and opened the conservatory door. As he was about to step inside, it occurred to him that the house may be fitted with a burglar alarm and he stepped back, muscles tense ready to run.

'The burglar alarm has been switched off,' said the voice.

'How did you know . . . ?' began Jack but then further comment was stifled as he was directed through the conservatory and into the house. He fumbled for a light switch in the dark hallway.

'No!' she bellowed in his ear, 'No lights!'

'But . . . .'

'Sorry Jack, no lights, I'll explain later.'

He peered up the stairway leading off the hall. Shadows cast by the streetlights outside flitted around the walls. He froze, half expecting the occupants of the house to appear on the landing.

'There's no one here,' said the voice reassuringly, 'the shadows are caused by the trees outside the landing window. When you reach the landing go through the first door on the right, there's a computer in there, switch it on.'

Unsteadily he made progress upstairs, noting with some alarm the display of wicked looking weapons mounted on the walls. Ceremonial swords, daggers and pistols prompted the unspoken question in his mind.

'My father collects them,' she said obligingly.

He was, by now, almost expecting to have his thoughts read and so the response came as no surprise.

He reached the landing and turned the door handle. Cautiously inching it open he put his head around the door and peered inside. His eyes had become more accustomed to the gloom enabling him to make out the shape of a computer sitting on a desk in the middle of the apparently large, empty, room. Slipping inside he pulled back the wheeled office chair and sat down uneasily at the desk. After considerable fumbling around, he found the on switch and the computer sprang into life.

The glow from the computer screen allowed him to survey the room in more detail. A steel filing cabinet was situated alongside the computer desk and on top of this was a ten inch statue of what looked like a Buddha, although it was difficult to be sure in the dim light. The only other furniture in the room was a large bookcase which filled a complete wall but was, strangely, empty. The curtains to the window, which he presumed overlooked the street, were closed. His attention was directed at the computer screen where, instead of the familiar start sequence text, there appeared rows of hieroglyphics, which he did not recognise. The screen then changed and a flashing cursor invited him to provide a password.

Jack pushed his fingers through his dark hair which became damp with the sweat from his brow. He shivered, more from anxiety than the cold. 'What do I do now?' he said shakily.

'Well done!' she said and quoted a sequence of numbers and letters. Fingers trembling, he entered the code as instructed.

'Now, there's a DVD under the statue; load it.'

There was a hint of excitement and relief in her voice as she emphasised the last two words. This served to heighten the tension Jack was already feeling. He looked around nervously as he inserted the DVD.

The MP3 Player began to crackle and he thought he heard what sounded like a faint sigh. He pushed the chair back from the desk and watched the screen intently, looking for some clue that may help him solve this mystery. Suddenly it dawned on him that the characters he had been watching looked like an oriental language. 'Maybe she's Chinese!' he said to himself.

At that moment the door was flung open violently. Startled, he swung around, the chair slipped from under him and he was tipped out of it with a crash. His head bumped heavily against the filing cabinet and he fell on the floor where he remained motionless.

CHAPTER 2

D.I. LIVINGSTONE SAT at his desk twiddling a pencil around in his fingers, pensively gazing at a picture of the Queen on the opposite wall. 'Where the devil is she?' he murmured, 'She can't have just disappeared.'

D.C. Collins shifted uncomfortably in his chair. This conversation had been re-enacted several times recently and he wasn't looking forward to another re-run, 'Buckingham Palace?' he ventured.

Livingstone ignored the remark and screwed his face into a scowl, his eyebrows converging into a single caterpillar like line across his forehead.

Collins tried to lift his boss's mood, 'Perhaps the Chinese authorities are mistaken,' he said hopefully, 'maybe she did get off the plane.'

'Maybe they're just not telling us,' retorted Livingstone disdainfully, 'anything from MI5?'

'No! They wouldn't tell us anything anyway.'

Livingstone nodded his agreement. The silence was strained, as though waiting for some sudden action.

He twiddled his pencil more vigorously, 'I saw her go through into the departure lounge with her father myself; funny little guy that one, I can't think why the F.O. thought he was a diplomat, more like a nutty professor.'

'Perhaps she can morph?' suggested Collins.

Livingstone shot him a dark look, 'You watch too much science fiction; in fact your whole life seems to be a fantasy.'

Chastened, Collins returned to his paperwork.

Livingstone stared at the telephone for a few moments then lunged towards it. Crashing his big fist on it, he expertly jerked the handset into the air and caught it neatly with the same hand. Collins jumped nervously. He hated that habit. He suspected his boss insisted on having an old type black handset, albeit with a digital keypad, for that reason as it was impossible to juggle in that way with a modern style handset.

Livingstone jabbed an aggressive finger at the buttons then bawled into the mouthpiece, 'Immigration?' There was a prolonged pause while he became more agitated.

'Have you found her yet?'

Collins could just make out the response and flinched, waiting for the explosion.

'How the hell could she get away? Don't you, and that bunch of morons you laughingly call "security", control access on the aircraft side of the terminal?' The voice pitch seemed to go up an octave in response, whereupon Livingstone threw the handset back on its cradle. 'She's not here, she's not there, so where the bloody hell is she?' he yelled to anyone who may want to listen. 'She's like the yellow bloody pimpernel.' Pleased with his literary adventure he flicked a screwed up ball of paper at Collins, 'Yellow pimpernel! Eh! Get it? Eh!

There followed a long pause, Collins busying himself with nonexistent paperwork as he waited for the next outburst.

'I think we need to take one more look at that house.'

'Well I suppose we haven't had the floorboards up yet,' muttered Collins sarcastically, bowing closer to his desk as if waiting for a blow. As he received no response he continued hopefully, 'I think Smiley is about ready to call it off.'

'Mm,' grunted Livingstone, 'Chief Superintendent Joan Wylie, alias Smiley, wonder woman of the Surveillance Unit. What does she know about anything?'

'That you work for her and not the other way round?'

'Smart arse!' growled Livingstone.

He slumped in his chair and drummed his fingers on the desk. 'She's in London somewhere, I can sense it, and this never fails.' He tapped his bulbous nose as if to emphasise its hidden talents. 'Trouble is, these chinks all look alike.'

Collins was used to the derogatory remarks flung about by his boss when dealing with other nationalities, 'We have her D.N.A. record,' he suggested.

'That's no good unless we know we have a fresh sample from the last two days,' grunted Livingstone.

Collins wilted into truculent silence, having pursued all the avenues his limited intellect would allow, while Livingstone rose from his desk and began to circle it, hands deep in his pockets, fingers jangling loose change.

'Come on "Boy Wonder"!' said Livingstone suddenly, and without waiting for a response grabbed car keys from his desk and left the office, trailing Collins in his wake.

. . . .

Jack began to regain consciousness. His head was throbbing and his mouth was dry. With blurred vision he attempted to survey the scene in front of him. His gaze was directed in the dim light to what appeared to be an erect paper clip, approximately four inches tall eyeing him from its vantage point on the edge of the desk. Dismissing this as an hallucination he was about to look around when the paper clip leaned forward, rolled its eyes and said, 'I'm Crip, may I herp you?'

Jack felt his mouth sag open. He felt nauseous and disorientated and was beginning to doubt his sanity. 'Oh! Clip,' he managed to repeat inanely through thick lips.

'No! Crip,' insisted the paper clip, pulling itself up to its full height, 'onelable generman won spell check?'

Jack's ability to think had temporarily deserted him so he didn't argue.

'Crip,' he repeated to himself softly.

He tried to feel the back of his head but realised his hands were tied behind his back. Shifting his body slightly, he could see enough by the light of the computer screen to guess that he was in the same position where he had fallen.

The noise of the computer keys clacking prompted him to shuffle into a sitting position with his back against the filing cabinet and look for the apparition but it had disappeared.

'You OK?' said a girl's voice.

'I think so, did you tie me up?'

'Just a precaution, a girl can't be too careful,' she said.

Jack guessed that the slight, attractive girl sitting at the computer was about nineteen, *but then*, he thought, *it is sometimes difficult to judge the age of Orientals*. Although she had some oriental features with straight black hair down to her waist, her small turned up nose and determined pointed chin suggested European influence in her lineage.

She was dressed in a baggy jumper, pale blue leggings cut off at the knee and scruffy trainers.

'I'm Lucy,' she said.

'Hello Lucy,' said the intrigued Jack, 'where did you come from? Are the girl in my MP3 Player?'

'Yes.'

'What happened?' he said, as she bent down to untie his hands.

'You fell over, you clumsy oaf.'

The smell of carbolic soap was unmistakable as she bent over him, and he found himself wondering why this pretty girl didn't wear perfume. The tension he had previously felt had been replaced by prickly irritation so he felt justified in some feeble retaliation at this insult.

'Well! Is that normally how you greet someone who saved you from . . . from . . . what exactly did I save you from?'

'I really am very grateful, you probably saved my life,' she said returning to the computer and continuing to type.

He got unsteadily to his feet, 'How did you do that thing with the MP3 Player?' he asked, 'And what is *that*?' He pointed an accusing finger at Crip who had re-appeared on top of the computer. The giant paper clip recoiled in shock and, with arms waving wildly fought to keep his balance, then slid off the back of the computer onto the floor with a metallic clunk.

'That's a long story. Let's just say he was our first success, so we're rather attached to him.'

With this, Crip pulled himself to his feet, bowed ceremoniously and winked. Jack stared in disbelief, bent down and extended a finger to assure himself that it was real. Crip avoided it, a frown appearing on his face.

'He's not been programmed for human contact,' explained Lucy, 'so he will avoid you.'

'But why is he called Crip?'

'Father named him, and trained him,' she said smiling at Jack's consternation.

'Ah, I see,' said Jack, hoping that one day he might. 'Is he real?'

'Oh yes! He's real all right, if a bit bizarre.' She paused, as if she were gauging the validity of her last statement; then continued, 'Sometimes, he gets too big for his boots, so I have to put him in his place, but he can be quite useful.' Crip looked hurt and lowered his eyelids as if waiting for a reprimand.

Her English was flawless, her voice musical and precise. Jack thought she was probably British with one Chinese parent and the naming of the paper clip possibly confirmed that her father was the Chinese half.

'Where are your parents?'

Lucy ignored the question, 'You are doing science at school?'

'A level Physics,' he replied. His mind was elsewhere, the response automatic.

'Good!' she said, 'At least it's a start.'

'Look, I've done you a favour the least you could do is to tell me what's going on,' he said casting a nervous glance in Crip's direction.

She pushed his MP3 Player across the desk, 'You won't need this in future.'

'In future?' he echoed.

'I shall communicate directly.'

'How? . . . Why? . . . Why me?'

'Because I selected *you*,' she said with a dismissive wave of her hand.

'For what?'

'Patience, I will explain.'

'And if I refuse to be selected?'

She slowly turned to face him and her face broke into an impish grin showing small, white, even teeth, 'You won't refuse. This is the most exciting opportunity of your life. For centuries the human race has only been able to dream of what is now possible. Now it is real and you will be involved from the beginning. If you are at all interested in science, you cannot refuse.'

'She light,' chimed Crip in a sing-song reedy little voice.

His mind was in turmoil, what would his parents say if they knew he had he been breaking into a house, and talking with a four inch paper clip? He needed time to think, but not here where she could manipulate him easily.

Gulping down his frustration he said, 'What do you want me to do?'

'Take me to McDonald's round the corner, I haven't eaten for two days, I'm starving.'

There had been no further opportunity for conversation. She had switched the computer to standby, whereupon Crip had vanished, thrown a heavy cloth over it, grabbed his hand and guided him through the darkened house.

'Why don't you put the lights on?' he enquired, but his question was met with silence.

The street lights reflected fluorescent orange on the still damp pavements as they half ran, half walked, to the McDonald's in a nearby street. She ordered enough food for two. Jack said he wasn't hungry, he was still feeling nauseous from his fall. He was becoming very concerned that his parents were expecting him home for tea and he was late. As he watched her eating he decided that conversation was impossible. He glanced at his watch, 'My parents are expecting me.'

'Go if you want,' she said through a mouthful of burger.

'But I thought you were going to explain?'

She pointed to her bulging mouth and shook her head, her eyes twinkling, obviously enjoying his distress.

'I thought you were exaggerating.'

Her eyes queried his comment.

'About not having eaten.'

She nodded.

'Mm . . . Mm . . . . Mf,' breadcrumbs and ketchup sprayed across the table.

'Hey, steady on!' he cried.

'Mm . . . Mm . . . Mf,' she continued.

He flicked a crumb from his shirt and held up his hand in surrender, 'OK I give in, don't try to speak, I'm just pleased you didn't have soup.'

She suddenly stopped mid bite, cleared her mouth and looked intently at him. 'Can I trust you Jack?' she said.

'You've already decided haven't you?'

'I want to hear it from you.'

He glanced around; they were almost alone in the restaurant. 'Well that's a fine question to ask someone who's just spent the last of his money trying to feed you,' he hissed. 'Tell me what all this is about, how you're doing these tricks and what you want from me!'

Her brown eyes softened slightly but continued to scan his face for clues. He had the uneasy feeling that he was being assessed for his future use and was beginning to resent it.

'Can I trust you Jack?' she repeated.

'I suppose so,' he said resignedly and then added peevishly, 'although you won't tell me what's going on.'

She had started eating again so conversation consisted of incomprehensible grunts.

Finally his frustration got the better of him, 'I've never known such a messy eater,' he complained, screwing up his face in disgust. Without warning she rolled a ball of soggy dough around in her mouth then spat it at him, hitting him full in the face. Flushed with anger, wounded pride and a smattering of ketchup, he jumped to his feet and made for the exit. With mild amusement she watched him go and then continued eating.

His anger began to subside as he strode home. The events of the day filled his mind with unanswered questions. Who was she? Where had she appeared from? He was sure that there was nobody in the house while he was operating the computer. Why had she needed him to help her, and what had he done? What was that paper clip thing, a hologram? As he walked up the path to his house the familiar surroundings began to press the problem into the back of his mind and the more mundane question of his parents' attitude to his future began to re-emerge. Maybe he had dreamed the whole thing anyway, some kind of self-hypnosis perhaps? One hand went to his pocket, the other to the back of his head. No he hadn't dreamed it; he had a painful lump on his head and no money!

Jack's father, a small portly balding man in his late forties noticed his worried expression.

'Is something wrong son? You look pale.'

'No, just had a difficult day at school,' said Jack.

'Well, I did say that it's not your thing . . . all this science stuff.'

'Dad! Please give it a rest, I don't need any more hassle, it's doing my head in.'

'Is that blood on your collar?' remarked his mother, rapidly changing the subject.

She was a small plump woman who had to stand on tiptoe in order to inspect his shirt. Instinctively Jack's hand went to cover the lump at the back of his head.

'Oh no, it's only ketchup,' she said, 'what have you been up to?'

He was saved from further questioning by his father: 'Megan's father's been round to see me.' He hesitated, waiting for some reaction, and then adjusted the half moon spectacles on his nose. Jack recognised the pompous courtroom pose and braced himself for what he knew was to come. 'He has alleged that you have started talking to your MP3 Player, how do you plead?' He cringed with embarrassment as his father addressed an imaginary jury.

Suddenly a thought occurred to him, *MP3 Player! Where is my MP3 Player? Oh no!* He'd left it at the house in their rush to get out.

His father was summing up, his face pink with pleasure at another case well won. Jack wasn't listening, his mind was racing. He would have to get it back, it was a present from his parents and they would be sure to notice it was missing.

'Stop going on at the boy,' said his mother in her homely way, 'he and Megan are bound to have their little tiffs from time to time.'

'Mum! We are not an item!'

It was no use, the more he protested the more she was convinced of the opposite. He could tell from her pursed lips, arms folded tightly across her chest stance, that further discussion would make things worse. Her round shape would deflect any adverse comment without consideration. Finally, he made some excuse about homework and escaped to his room.

He sat for some time on the end of his bed staring at the blank wall. His mother had him married to Megan and settled down with a family. His father had decided he was to study law and become a solicitor in his firm. They didn't seem to care what he wanted and weren't even prepared to listen to him. He could feel the seeds of discontent stirring within him and knew that in time this would grow into a full scale falling out with them.

Now! This thing with the intriguing, mysterious Lucy! His gaze shifted to his television which he had automatically switched on when he entered his bedroom. Nothing in his boring, humdrum, predictable life could have prepared him for what had happened. She was right, it was exciting! He ruefully fingered the lump on the back of his head and thought about her. How was she able to do the things that she did? He resolved to return to the house tomorrow and get to the bottom of the mystery. 'I have to anyway,' he said to himself, 'I have to get my MP3 Player back!'

The wall was providing no answers so he settled down to do his homework and immersed himself in the equally weird world of quantum mechanics.

CHAPTER 3

'JACK! WAKE UP!'

'Ugh! Whassamarrer?'

He opened one eye, raised himself onto his elbows and surveyed his bedroom. Everything lay where he had dropped it on the previous evening. He had fallen asleep without switching off his bedside light or television. At first he thought it was his mother's voice preparing to scold him about the mess but as he awoke he realised he was alone. The events of yesterday were hazy and so it was a profound shock when the TV blank screen suddenly took on the shape of a familiar face.

'Jack I want to talk to you.'

'Lucy! How . . . do you do that?'

She winked at him from the TV screen, 'Like it? Do you think I would make a good newsreader, or weather girl perhaps?' The look of astonishment on his face made her giggle.

'Look, I'm sorry I walked out on you yesterday, it's just that . . . ,' he began.

Her face suddenly became serious, 'Forget it, it really doesn't matter.'

He looked at his watch, it was four a.m.

'Your room is an absolute shambles, I've never seen such a mess,' she teased.

'Have you made a pact with the Devil?' he groaned. 'Hey, wait a minute . . . can you see everything in my room?'

'Everything,' she chuckled.

He jumped out of bed to arrange things in a more acceptable heap, only to realise that he was naked. He blushed and pulled the bedclothes around himself.

'Mm,' she giggled, 'not bad.'

'This is awful,' muttered Jack, 'a bloke can't get any privacy at all.' He grabbed the TV remote controller and switched to a different channel. She reappeared, her eyes dancing with excitement at his alarm.

'Don't switch off,' she said, 'I promise I'll be good.'

He hesitated, finger hovering over the off button.

'Please!' she said with an endearing smile.

'Well, I suppose you would find another way to pester me,' he relented.

'Now you're getting the idea,' she said, 'the thing is, I need some money.'

'Ah! So it's extortion. That's what's at the bottom of all this.' He scrabbled under the bedclothes for the controller which he had dropped earlier.

'Don't switch off Jack!'

'I think you're a witch. Anyway I can't help you because you ate all the money I had last night.'

The screen went momentarily blank and what then appeared made him gasp in astonishment.

'How . . . did you get . . . that?' he stammered, 'And what have you done to it?'

'It was quite easy,' she said triumphantly, 'I used the internet to get your student account and then put some money into it.'

He gaped at the screen. His meagre savings had ballooned to over five thousand pounds.

'You can't do that . . . it's just a copy isn't it?'

'No! It's authentic alright.'

'Where did the money come from?'

'It's mine; I just can't get at it in the normal way.'

'Why is everything about you . . . different?' he said struggling for words. 'Why can you never do anything in the normal way?'

'Trust me Jack, I am quite normal, it's just my circumstances which are different.'

'But if five thousand pounds suddenly appears in my student account, someone will start asking questions, won't they?'

'Don't worry it won't be in there for very long but if they do, you have a rich auntie who has taken pity on a poor struggling student, it happens all the time.'

'Oh no,' he groaned, feeling helpless, 'what do you want me to do?'

'I want you to buy me a top of the range laptop and some accessories to go with it.'

'Why can't you buy one?'

'The truth is I don't exist. So you see it would be difficult for me to buy anything.'

'Don't be silly, of course you exist. If you don't exist how did you tie me up, spit in my face, trough like a pig in McDonald's and captivate me? Are you a hologram like that crazy paperclip and am I now talking to myself?'

Lucy's face became sad and wistful.

'Have I said something wrong?'

'Not exactly,' she said, 'it's not my intention to captivate you Jack, you are your own person I have no call on you.

When the time is right I will explain. Try to be patient. You are the only person who can help me,' she pleaded.

He felt the urge to continue the conversation but saw from the determined look on her face that she would not expand on what she had just said.

'Sleep well Jack, I'll call you soon,' she chimed, 'and *do* clean up your room.'

There was a soft click and she was gone, leaving him, once more, with a spinning head. Whatever did she mean when she said she didn't exist? Was it all a dream? Once more he fingered the lump at the back of his head. *How did I get this then?*

CHAPTER 4

LIKE A PAIR of bloodhounds Livingstone and Collins sniffed around the ground floor of number fourteen, but found nothing.

'Just as we left it,' said Collins morosely, 'she can't be living here.'

'Check the toilet cistern upstairs,' ordered Livingstone.

'Why?'

'To see if the dye's been flushed away,' he said with a loud sigh and a long suffering look.

Livingstone continued examining the empty rooms as the sound of the toilet flushing drifted downstairs.

'No! He can't have,' he gasped, as he dragged his bulk upstairs.

A sheepish Collins emerged from the bathroom, 'Sorry I just had to go.'

'And did you notice what colour the water was?' said the purple faced policeman.

'Well no, I didn't think to.'

Seeing Livingstone's mounting anger, he scuttled into the front bedroom. 'Hey, look at this chief,' he yelled, 'jackpot!' Livingstone gave a low whistle at the reason for his excitement.

'Now, I wonder who can have switched that computer on?' he exclaimed. 'That clinches it, she's got to be around here somewhere, unless . . . , are you sure you switched it off the last time we were here?'

Collins looked hurt. 'I . . . I . . . think so chief,' he stuttered.

A faint metallic scuffling in the corner of the darkened room suddenly distracted both men.

'What's that?' exclaimed Livingstone.

'Dunno.'

'Well go and check it out!' he bellowed.

Nervously, Collins edged towards the location of the noise.

'Bloody hell!' he exclaimed as the source of the noise disappeared under the heavy bookcase.

'Well what is it?'

'I reckon it was a paper clip, about four inches high. It was a paper clip body with arms and legs. It dropped on all fours and ran under there,' remarked Collins excitedly, crouching on his hands and knees and attempting to peer under the bookcase.

'I will accept what you saw was a mouse,' retorted Livingstone with a pained expression, 'a paper clip, particularly with arms and legs, is a figment of your overheated imagination.'

'But chief,' protested the unfortunate man, 'I saw it, it disappeared under the bookcase.' He began to pull ineffectually at the heavy piece of furniture.

'Give us a hand.'

Livingstone stood over him, watching his futile efforts dispassionately.

'Get up! You born again flatfoot, what you saw was a mouse, OK?'

Collins jumped to his feet brushing his shock of red hair out of his wild, staring eyes. Livingstone ignored his obvious state of distress and waving his hand at the computer growled, 'Switch that bloody thing off and check the rest of the house.'

Collins shuffled over to the computer, furtively checking the floor as he went; 'Paper clip,' he muttered under his breath. As he sat down he noticed the DVD lying on the filing cabinet and quickly inserted it.

'Don't touch that!' yelled Livingstone, but it was too late. The Chinese hieroglyphs were flashing across the screen then pausing, as the programme requested a password.

'Out with it,' sniffed Livingstone, sensing that Collins was troubled by what he saw.

'Have the boffins seen this?'

'Yes they gave it a clean bill of health, said they could find nothing on it.'

'So why would you password protect something if there was nothing on it?' enquired Collins.

Livingstone didn't want to get dragged into a conversation about which he knew nothing, particularly with this fresh faced newly promoted detective constable. The last thing he needed was a lecture from a computer nerd. 'If they say there's nothing on it, then there's nothing on it' he rasped. 'Take the dammed thing out, switch off, and call in the fingerprint boys.'

A further detailed search of the whole building proved to be fruitless, so two hours later they were in Livingstone's office awaiting the results of the fingerprint analysis, but no further forward.

The mystery deepened when the results came. One fresh set of fingerprints had been found, but they were not those of the Chinese girl. Livingstone scratched his head and glowered at Collins. 'Were you wearing marigolds?'

Collins nodded and produced the thin rubber gloves from his desk drawer.

'It might have been vandals who broke in and tried the computer,' mused Livingstone.

'But there was no sign of a break in,' said Collins, 'vandals with a key? Maybe she has an accomplice.'

'I have the impression that she's a quirky loner, but you may be right. All right smart boy,' said Livingstone, 'I'm going to report to Smiley and see what her take is on this one.'

Joan Wylie sat impassively behind her desk and scrutinised the shabby figure in front of her critically. She was a middle-aged career policewoman with the personality of a glacier; cold, relentless and with the ability to crush any obstacle in her path. Her famous grimace inspired terror and respect among young constables who had nicknamed her "Smiley". Being a highly intelligent woman, she was aware of this and frequently used it to her own advantage. Her chiselled features and rimless spectacles gave her a severe appearance which she now used to good effect on the hapless Livingstone. She frowned and allowed her ice blue eyes to bore into him. Livingstone flinched. She seemed to know he was bordering on insubordination before he even opened his mouth. Pension uppermost in his mind, he decided to err on the side of caution.

'We seem to have lost her Ma'am,' he said ruefully.

Smiley's frown deepened, 'Unfortunate,' she muttered, 'I expect a detailed report of your carelessness Livingstone; misplacing suspects is a serious matter. Do you remember, perhaps, when you last had her in your possession?' she said with more than a hint of sarcasm.

'At Heathrow Ma'am, we released her into the departure lounge.'

'And she didn't arrive in China?'

'No Ma'am.'

'So what do I tell the Minister?'

'Minister, Ma'am?'

'Yes Livingstone. Minister! This person is a threat to our national security.'

Livingstone's eyes widened in alarm, 'But she's only an nineteen year old kid.'

'Nevertheless, my instructions are clear, D.I. Livingstone, and so are yours. If she didn't arrive in China, she must still be here . . . , on our patch. Find this young lady now, failure is not an option.'

'Yes Ma'am,' he said sheepishly, turning on his heel and leaving her office.

CHAPTER 5

T HE NEXT DAY at school Jack made his way to the computer room with Dipper, his best friend.

'What do you know about number fourteen?' he said tentatively as they sat down at their respective computers.

Dipper looked at him blankly. He had the appearance of a typical bookworm with owlish eyes peering through bottle glass spectacles in a plump, fast food ravaged face. His hair was an untidy mousey mat in danger of covering his entire upper face and his protruding lower lip gave him a permanent truculent appearance.

Theirs was an unlikely alliance which had grown from a mutual requirement in their early days at Greystone. Dipper had come to Jack's assistance with the trickier parts of calculus, while Jack's friendship had provided Dipper with some protection from the ever present threat of bullying. It was now very rare for Dipper to be intimidated, for everyone knew that the captain of the school football team, the six foot muscular, super-fit Jack was hovering in the background. On the whole it worked well, but like any relationship it did spawn occasional misunderstandings.

'Was this maths homework I forgot?' he intoned, worry creeping into his voice.

'No you idiot,' retorted Jack, 'the house, number fourteen, just down the street.'

'Better than thirteen?' replied the confused Dipper, 'I suppose it's not quite as unlucky.'

'Megan reckons it's haunted.'

'Megan's an air head,' he responded sharply.

By now both the boys had switched on their computers and were preparing to log on to the internet. Jack's computer had hung up when suddenly the help screen appeared with the helpful paper clip. This paper clip, however, was very different; it was wearing a mandarin robe!

Jack gave a startled cry, 'Crip!'

'What's crap?' muttered Dipper, leaning over to peer at his screen.

'Nothing,' said Jack, hurriedly dismissing Crip from view.

As Dipper turned back to his own computer a message flashed onto Jack's screen, it read: "Don't tell him anything or I might have to roast your eyeballs on a spit. This is something witches in China do when they curse their victims, Love Lucy." Jack was stunned; she didn't really mean that, did she? He decided not to risk it; after all he reasoned, you don't mess with a witches curse and she seemed capable of anything.

Dipper resumed the conversation, 'Why the interest?'

'Interest?' said Jack vaguely.

'In number fourteen,' said Dipper, who was now beginning to wonder how the conversation had started, and why.

'Oh just Megan trying to upset me I suppose,' he replied.

'You want to watch out for that one,' said Dipper, crinkling his nose in feigned disgust, 'she's got the nesting instinct big time, and she's definitely got you in her sights.'

This was punctuated with the short staccato rattling of his computer keys while Jack marvelled at the speed and accuracy of his typing.

Jack lapsed into silence his forehead furrowed and lips pursed. He had to get to the bottom of this. Lucy was making his life even more complicated. His friend, blissfully unaware of Jack's change of mood kept up a one sided chatter throughout break, accepting the occasional grunt from Jack as his part in the conversation.

All the teachers noted Jack's lack of attention in their lessons. He also had the uneasy impression that Megan was watching him very carefully. During the course of the day his mind wandered back and forth over the events of the previous day. Who is Lucy? Where are her parents? How did she communicate with him through his MP3 Player and television? Why was she doing this? There were so many unanswered questions swimming through his mind in confusing repetition.

'Why me?' he suddenly blurted out loud, in the Physics lesson.

'Why not?' answered the ever-attentive Megan eagerly swinging round in her chair.

Smithy grunted and peered over his glasses.

'Young man,' he began, pointing a chewed pencil at Jack for emphasis, 'you seem to be in some distress.'

This created more interest throughout the class than a simple rebuke. Everyone turned to examine the *distress* in more detail. Jack responded by blushing as he became the object of suppressed laughter.

'Onto more important things,' continued Smithy as Jack tried to hide his confusion and embarrassment. With the exception of Megan, the class resumed their studies.

She continued to view Jack's discomfort with a heart full of compassion and longing.

'Ahem!' Smithy grunted again and she quickly turned around.

Feeling the eyes of the world were upon him, he attempted to make himself inconspicuous which for a boy of six foot was difficult. He closed his eyes and wished for the end of the school day. The loss of his MP3 Player worried him greatly and he determined to retrieve it from the house on his way home that evening.

'What was all that about?' said Dipper later, 'I thought Megan was going to jump on you there and then.'

Jack laughed nervously, 'Oh, nothing I've just got something on my mind. Do your parents tell you what you're going to do when you leave school?'

'No! They're pretty good like that; they're leaving that up to me. They just want me to go to University and decide for myself from there.'

'You do realise,' said Jack, poking him in his premature paunch, 'that you'll only be able to live on marmite and toast when you go there.'

Dipper gave him a knowing wink, 'I'll get a part time job in a restaurant.'

'You always have an answer,' chuckled Jack.

He felt much better, later, as he swung out of the school gates, his athletic frame braced against the cold north-easterly wind, he set off down the road with purpose. He was going to solve this once and for all; he would confront Lucy and insist on an explanation.

He boldly knocked on the front door of number fourteen several times, while glancing around and hoping he had given Megan the slip. There was no reply. Screwing up his courage he went around to the rear of the house, retrieved the key from under the water butt and entered the conservatory. Quickly finding his way upstairs he went into the computer room but could not see his MP3 Player anywhere. He searched the filing cabinet drawers without success then sat down at the computer to think if he should begin to search the rest of the house. He had noticed that everything was covered in a fine dust, 'Like talcum powder,' he said aloud. He switched on the computer, loaded the DVD and watched the Chinese characters dancing on the screen.

'You wan some herp,' chimed a tinny little voice as Crip appeared on the screen. Suddenly he had an idea, perhaps he could find out what he wanted to know from Crip.

'Yes! Where are Lucy's parents?'

Crip rolled his eyes at this unexpected question. 'Have searched database, cannot find answer,' came the mechanical response.

Jack thought for a minute; obviously personal questions were off limits. He decided to change his approach.

'How do you work?'

Crip looked pleased; this was a question he wanted to answer. The screen went momentarily blank then a Word text document appeared. Jack glanced at the number of pages, over forty thousand! So much for that enquiry he thought. Crip reappeared looking very pleased with himself.

'You lead?' he said.

'No I don't think so,' said Jack, 'well at least not in this lifetime.'

Crip looked despondent, 'you no won know how Crip work?'

'Not in that sort of detail, thank you Crip.'

Suddenly Lucy's face appeared on the screen, Jack started back from the computer, 'You're not pleased to see me?' she said impishly.

'Well yes,' he said doubtfully, 'you just startled me.'

'Well, I am *very* pleased to see *you*, thank goodness you forgot your MP3 Player yesterday.'

'I don't understand,' he cried, 'I don't understand anything anymore.'

'OK let me see if I can help you, is this what you were looking for?'

His MP3 Player suddenly materialised on the desk in front of him! He gaped stupidly for a few seconds then tentatively reached out a finger to touch it. 'It's real!' he gasped, 'Not a hologram.'

Crip collapsed at the bottom of the screen in a fit of tinny cackling.

'You *are* a witch!'

'I'll pretend you didn't say that,' she said with a chuckle, 'now type in this number and go downstairs into the conservatory.'

He obediently followed her instruction and made his way downstairs through the darkened house. His whole body was tingling with excitement and anticipation as he stood in the conservatory wondering if she would perform more magic.

He was beginning to despair of anything happening when a faint blue wisp of light began to drift around the conservatory. He examined the room and concluded there was no other source of light for this wraith to pick up its illumination. He stepped back to avoid contact with the ethereal entity. The light began to rotate and form a vortex at the centre of the room. He stared in astonishment as the vortex assumed the shape of a sphere.

His stomach was urging him to run, but his head ensured he remained transfixed. The glowing blue sphere began to grow in the centre of the room, floating a metre above the floor, iridescent in the gathering dusk. He peered into the glowing ball of light more closely but could see nothing identifiable. He tenuously stretched out a finger and allowed the tip to penetrate the surface then rapidly withdrew it as it began to vibrate and tingle. The sphere expanded rapidly to the size where it could swallow him up, so he stepped back smartly, It began to pulsate slowly at first, then more rapidly. Interlaced fine lines of brighter colour appeared on the surface like a myriad of spiders' webs. These began to vibrate independently from the oscillations of the sphere. The whole thing was happening in complete silence however he could feel the tension building to a grand climax. Instinctively he ducked as the globe gave a violent shake followed by a soft phut! Lucy stepped out of the sphere.

'Anti climax isn't it?' she remarked as she stepped forward briskly.

CHAPTER 6

'I'VE NOTICED OUR Jack's been a bit dreamy of late, haven't you Dad?' Betty Dawkins glanced expectantly across the comfortable but unremarkable lounge at her husband. She had been trying to engage him in conversation on this subject for two days with little success.

'Growing pains,' he grunted, hoping to deflect the unwanted attention and shook his paper as if to underline the finality of his statement. Betty was not to be deflected, determined as she was to obtain her husband's agreement on the matter of Jack's future.

'He doesn't show a lot of interest in girls; and that Megan's such a nice girl,' she said with a sigh.

Laying his spectacles and newspaper down on the table beside him, he said reluctantly, 'Give him time, he's only just seventeen. When he's old enough he'll join the firm, find himself a nice girl and settle down.'

She looked doubtful, 'He seems more interested in science than law.'

'Oh he's young yet, he doesn't understand. He's bound to have these fads from time to time.'

'Well you don't seem to have noticed,' she said, 'but he's doing 'A' level Physics, I would hardly call that a fad.'

'He'll change his mind when he goes to university, he'll come round, you'll see.'

'You can't be sure of that.'

'When he realises that there's much less money in science, he'll change his mind.'

Betty was agitated. She stood up and walked around the lounge. 'So you think he'll be attracted by this magnificent lifestyle,' she said sarcastically, waving an arm at her surroundings.

Nigel was stung by the implied criticism and stared at his wife angrily, 'You've had no reason to complain.'

Betty pursed her lips and sat down again, 'I don't understand it Nigel, you're a senior partner in a respected law firm and yet . . . ,' her voice trailed away nervously as if she were treading on hallowed ground, 'we don't seem to see any benefit,' she concluded. The words tumbled out of her mouth unbidden. She immediately regretted the outburst and hastily turned back to the safety of her knitting.

Nigel returned to his newspaper but the typeface was invisible to him. He was thinking hard, mentally checking the façade he had carefully constructed over the years for any clues she could have uncovered. Satisfied that he had left no loopholes, he relaxed and continued the conversation, 'We will see the benefit when we retire. My pension will enable us to see the world in luxury,' he said.

Her knitting needles clacked for a few seconds then stopped abruptly. 'How do you think he and Megan are getting on?' she asked.

'Well if what Megan's father told me was true; not very well,' he said.

'It's most unlike Jack to be rude to anybody,' she said thoughtfully.

'What I don't understand,' began Nigel, 'is how those parents,' he waved a vague arm in the direction of Megan's house, 'can have produced such a lovely girl.'

'They're all right, a bit rough perhaps,' she said defensively.

'Rough? That man's an out and out crook, and as for her, how anyone can appear in public looking like that is beyond me. If you had your way you would have Jack married off to Megan. Can you imagine what the wedding reception would be like? Half the criminal fraternity of North London would be there . . . and me, a respectable solicitor!'

Betty, however, could only see the romantic vision of her handsome son and the beautiful Megan in white wedding dress, standing on the church steps as man and wife. 'Even so, they would make a lovely couple if you could ignore her parents.'

'How could you ignore them? We would almost be related. No it's not on, you mustn't encourage it. I don't want to be seen associating with that man, or his family.'

Betty was startled by the fierceness of Nigel's comment. 'So you can tell him what his career is going to be, but I can't help him make the right decision when it comes to affairs of the heart?'

Nigel grimaced and picked up his paper again. He didn't want this conversation any more. Betty bit her lip. She noticed that although he appeared to be reading the paper, his spectacles remained on the table.

'I thought I heard him talking to himself in the early hours of the morning.' offered Nigel from behind the paper, to avoid a strained silence.

'I wonder if he's under some sort of stress that he's not telling us about,' replied Betty anxiously.

'He's got nothing to worry about, it's all sorted, I've had it all agreed,' he retorted sharply, ramming his spectacles on his nose and shaking the paper vigorously.

'I shall be going out to my club later,' he said.

Betty nodded a mute response. *Another late night,* she thought.

. . . .

'Fantastic!' said Jack when they reached the computer room, his eyes still wide with amazement, 'That was some trick.'

Lucy eyed him critically; she was still not sure. 'That was the most advanced science you are ever likely to be privileged to see,' she said frostily, 'not a trick!'

Jack noted the seriousness of her expression, her jaw firmly set, eyes boring unblinkingly into his, and made a mental note to curb his childish outbursts in the future.

'What was it?' he said tentatively.

For what seemed an age to Jack, Lucy's pretty face was screwed in an expression of intense concentration as she struggled to find a way of explaining her situation. Finally she sat down at the computer and swung around to face him.

'My father is a Professor of Physics at Beijing University. Twenty years ago he was invited to the University in London to further his research into quantum mechanics. Do you know anything about quantum mechanics?'

Jack thought for a moment then recalled a lesson at school, 'Oh yes I remember,' he said, 'that's the weird bit of physics where nuclear billiard balls can't make up their mind whether they're waves, like radio waves, or particles.'

'What do you know about quantum computers?' she asked.

'Nothing! Is that what this is?' he said pointing to the computer on the desk.

'Yes.'

'So what's the difference between this and a normal computer?'

'Well,' she replied warming to her subject, 'a quantum computer can do hundreds of thousands of calculations all at the same time, which is far superior to a normal computer.'

'I don't see any advantage in that,' he said, 'you can only use one answer at any time.'

'It's not necessarily answers we're interested in,' replied Lucy, 'often it's the state of each calculation superimposed with all the rest at any given moment in time, which is useful.'

Jack felt he was out of his depth and struggling already. 'Why is that?' he asked, hoping for an easy answer.

'Well, this is a great simplification,' she said, 'but my father's research has proved that this is how the human brain works.'

He had to concede now that he was utterly lost.

'So what does that do for you?'

'The ability to generate ideas artificially, and to map and describe in quantum terms the ideas present in a brain at any given instant.'

'Just a minute,' he interrupted, 'aren't there billions of nerve cells in the brain, how could you possibly map all that lot?'

'You're right! Fortunately we don't have to. All we have to map are what we call *attractors*, which determine the state of consciousness at any time, not the state of each neuron.'

'I don't understand,' he said perching on the edge of the computer desk, 'what are attractors?'

'Imagine a shoreline,' she continued, 'the sea will be affected by its environment, part of which is the sea-bed and the prevailing winds. The effect of this is to set up eddies and small whirl pools which, although dynamic in themselves, are almost permanent while the environment stays roughly the same. These whirlpools and eddies can be thought of as attractors in the seascape, and the same can be said of areas of activity in the brain. Altogether these areas make up your personality, or the way you respond to your environment. When the environment changes, your brain learns to respond and modify your attractor landscape for optimum benefit. The sea also changes in response to environmental change, but, because it's not conscious, it's not a learning experience.'

Jack's mind had gone numb in response to this barrage of new ideas. He folded his arms and sat on the desk slowly shaking his head, struggling to understand. 'So it's not as complex as mapping billions of neurons, or the state of little bits of information.'

'Remember the atoms of your body have changed many times since your childhood, but the essence of you hasn't been affected by that. The atoms and neurons, in themselves, don't contribute to consciousness,' explained Lucy, 'the *relationships* between them and their constant information transactions with the environment, determine consciousness. It's that information which we map and use.

'How do you know all this stuff?'

'I learned a lot from my father from being very small, I was interested and he is very patient. He discovered a way of using a quantum computer, with relatively little computer memory, to map consciousness at any time. The other important factor is the Chinese written language, it makes it much easier to programme.'

He was startled to hear that, 'I thought there were thousands of characters in the Chinese language, how can that make programming easier?'

'What we're dealing with is consciousness, which is about ideas, and the Chinese written language, although it has about six thousand basic characters, is also representing ideas, that's what each character is, an idea or icon. Six thousand states to a parallel quantum computer is chicken feed.'

Jack's brain was buzzing. Although he really didn't understand much of what she had said, he found himself remarking, 'I suppose ideas are the result of parallel thoughts all superimposed at the quantum level.'

'There you see! I knew I'd made the right decision when I picked you.' Lucy flashed her even white teeth in a big smile.

'But I still don't see why you use Chinese instead of English,' he said. 'After all there are only twenty six characters to deal with in English.'

'The Chinese language gives us a direct representation of an idea or thought, whereas with English you have to go through another transformation to arrive at the same result. Using a combination of twenty six letters, for each letter of each word required to express that idea, you perform a factorial calculation which can result in making a selection from more possibilities than there are atoms in the universe. In Chinese you get the result in the blink of an icon.'

This was one step too far for him. He launched himself from the edge of the desk walked around the room with an intense frown on his face as he tried to make sense of it all.

'What you see when the computer starts is a programme, or algorithm written in Chinese' said Lucy. With that she started up the computer again and loaded the DVD. The dancing Chinese characters appeared on the screen. 'This sets up the condition for the portal,' she explained.

'So where does this portal lead?'

'To other dimensions,' she said mysteriously.

'Other dimensions?' echoed Jack. 'This gets crazier by the second. You'll be telling me next that Mr. Spock is your spirit guide.'

'Jack, you will have to learn to restrain yourself. When I threatened to cast a spell on you . . . , I meant it. I can do something similar to a spell by changing your consciousness . . . although I do stop short of turning people into frogs. There can be no flippancy here. This is serious. You have witnessed this for yourself. To access other dimensions you have to lose your physical body and become pure consciousness, or if you like, in your terms, spirit. As for Doctor Spock there's no room for child psychologists in this discipline.'

'No! *Mr* Spock. "Star Trek"?'

She gave him a blank stare and raised a warning finger.

Jack's blood ran cold. She was serious! What added weight to the menace was the cold, purposeful manner in which it she had delivered it.

'I then put in my personal identification which primes the computer to receive my consciousness through a system called quantum entanglement, or EPR,' she continued calmly, as if her threat had never existed.

He was barely listening now, as the possible uses of the science she was describing began to take shape in his mind and he realised why she was being so severe with him.

Of course, he thought, *the military implications of this are enormous. Transporting whole armies through a portal in an instant or delivering a nuclear device to an enemy through a portal!* He now realised that he was involved in something that could be extremely dangerous for both of them. He dimly heard her say, 'I can dissipate my material atoms anywhere and provided I retain the relationships which exist between them, along with the gene pattern which is exclusive to me, I can reconstitute myself.'

Whose side is she on? China? Europe? America? Can I trust her? Do I have any choice?

'However I do need the computer to be switched on when I am in other dimensions. If the computer has been switched off for some reason, I need someone to type in the password, as I have no physical means to do this.'

'And that's where I come in,' said Jack, emerging from his private thoughts.

'Exactly,' agreed Lucy.

'When you spoke to me on my MP3 Player yesterday . . . ,' he began.

'I was stuck in the fifth dimension,' she interrupted, answering the unspoken question, 'and the computer had been turned off.'

'Why was the computer switched off? Nobody else can get into this house can they?'

She hesitated, 'I don't know, maybe there had been a power cut.'

'But,' he protested, 'if there had been a power cut the main switch would have still have been on and the computer would have come back on when the power returned.'

She shrugged her shoulders dismissively, 'I don't think it works like that,' she said lamely.

'What if I don't want to help you?' he said.

Lucy paused while she decided her approach. 'You don't realise this but I know why you have a difficult relationship with your parents. I know that if you don't stand up for yourself, your father will decide your future for you, and you will never realise your potential. How could you refuse this opportunity to involve yourself at the cutting edge of scientific discovery?' She reached over and enclosed his hand in both of hers, they were warm and comforting. 'I also know the sort of person you are; honest, dependable, caring and loyal. I picked you for these and many other reasons; you are intelligent, willing to learn, fit and attractive, but most of all, I picked you because I need a partner, I need you!'

Lucy watched him flush with pleasure at this last comment. She knew she had achieved her objective and pressed home her advantage: 'You can choose a boring predictable life as a family solicitor married to someone like Megan, or you can place your trust in me and have an exciting rewarding adventure. You've already seen some of what can be done, so now it's not possible for you to go back.'

'So you've been spying on me,' he protested limply.

'I had no choice, what we are dealing with is far bigger than the wounded pride of any individual.'

'What about the politics of all this?' he said tentatively.

She understood his dilemma immediately; 'This is for the good of science and all humanity.'

'That's all very idealistic,' he said, 'but what happens when the military realise the possibilities?'

'We have to maintain control over it and that requires absolute secrecy . . . ,' she began, then, her face became grim and set as she noticed the computer screen.

'Jack, we didn't switch off the portal and there's someone in the conservatory,' she said in a hoarse whisper. 'Go down quickly and see who's there.'

He half ran, half stumbled, down the dim staircase and flung open the conservatory door. It was empty.

He raced back upstairs, 'No one there,' he panted.

Lucy swung round to the computer and began typing rapidly. For several minutes she frantically rattled the keyboard and said nothing, while Jack shifted uneasily on the edge of the desk, desperately wondering what was going on but afraid to disturb her concentration by asking. Finally she stopped typing slumped forward slightly in the chair and with a sigh said, 'I think you'll find her in the conservatory now, you'd better take her home; and Jack?'

'Yes?'

'Don't forget your MP3 Player,' she said pushing it across the desk towards him, Jack picked it up and slipped it in his pocket. He hurried back to the conservatory, dreading what he might find.

Gathering his courage he swung open the inner door and saw a dim shape of someone lying on the floor. It was Megan! He bent over her and tested for her pulse, 'Thank goodness,' he gasped, 'she's alive.' Lifting and half dragging her he managed to manoeuvre her to the front of the house and into the glare of the streetlights. He sat her down on the low stone wall in front of the garden and supported her as she regained consciousness.

'Wha . . . what happened,' she mumbled, her eyes flickering open momentarily.

Wondering how much she may have seen and remembered, he opted for a cautious approach. 'I think you must have fainted,' he said quickly, 'come on let's get you home.' It suddenly occurred to him that Lucy had said "you'll find *her*". Did she know it was Megan?

'But I never faint,' she protested drowsily.

'Well you did this time.'

'Was I behind you,' she said standing up and swaying.

'Yes.'

'So how did you know?'

'Know what?'

'That I'd fainted, idiot.'

'I think you must have shouted out before you fainted,' he said limply.

In her confused state she seemed satisfied with this answer and began to walk, allowing herself to be supported by him. At last she was close to him and if she had to faint to do it; ah well! So be it!

It was clear to him that she remembered nothing of whatever she had experienced in the conservatory.

. . . .

Megan's bedroom was fairly severe for a teenage girl, reflecting her practical, forthright personality. There were few items which indicated femininity. The wallpaper, which was her parent's choice, was a heavy floral pattern. She would have preferred something less fussy. It was to this that her attention was drawn as she lay in bed the following morning and slowly became aware of her surroundings. It had been a habit of hers for years to stare at the floral pattern and imagine faces in the half light of dawn, and this morning was no exception. Her mind drifted back to the events of the previous evening; why had she fainted? She lay enjoying the memory of being close to Jack on the way home. He had shown concern for her welfare and she drew some encouragement from that, although his final remark was curious, "try to forget it had happened", he had said. Naturally as she could remember little except for the walk home, arm in arm with Jack, she assumed he was referring to their first real intimacy. It didn't really make sense. As she pondered over this, hovering between fully awake and daydreaming, she became aware of low indistinct voices murmuring. It seemed to come from the top corner of her room. Try as she might she could not understand the words, it was like two people whispering together conspiratorially in a foreign language. She began to feel fear gripping and squeezing at her stomach and tried to tell herself in her pragmatic way to stop been stupid, it must be the sound of leaves rustling in the wind on the large beech tree outside her window. She tried to shut it out of her mind and concentrated on the flower patterns on the wallpaper instead. They seemed to be shimmering, fuzzy around the edges while the surface of the wall was clear and distinct. Megan blinked furiously, snuggled further down in the bed, then shut her eyes. After a short while she peered at the flower patterns again. The indistinct outline had become hard and recognisable. She shuddered with horror as she realised her previously imagined faces had become real! And they began to move! She watched in paralysed terror as a thousand little unblinking black eyes stared at her from the walls. She tried to force out the scream but it jammed in her throat, her muscles tightened around it until she thought she was going to choke, and then, the evil grinning faces slowly began to slide down the walls and slither across the carpet towards her.

CHAPTER 7

O<small>N</small> S<small>ATURDAY</small> <small>MORNING</small> Lucy and Jack made an early start. Lucy knew exactly what she wanted from the computer shop and pointed it out to Jack who then had it demonstrated by an assistant, while she waited outside. He paid for the laptop by cheque, fervently hoping the size of it would not attract the wrong kind of attention to his student account. As they approached Lucy's house Jack began to express doubts which had been clouding his mind.

'What happened to Megan?' he ventured.

'She walked into the portal by mistake, she's just a nosey nuisance,' added Lucy.

'Will she be alright?'

'I don't see why not,' she said curtly, 'did she remember anything?'

'No.'

'Good,' she said with a finality that suggested she wanted no further conversation on the subject.

'I think I'll go round to her house and see how she is,' he said, after a short pause.

'If you must, but I still haven't finished telling you about my situation,' she said, slightly peeved.

'I'll come straight around after I've made sure she's OK.'

Lucy didn't reply and her sudden coldness left Jack feeling a little perplexed as he took a detour to Megan's house.

Megan's mother greeted him on the doorstep. Jack mentally recoiled at this large, big boned woman, dressed in a vivid purple dress with orange cardigan and support stockings, finished off with animal head slippers. Her hair sported two large pink rollers at the front followed by a rampant frizzy bush of hair at the rear, all framing a sagging but cheerful face. He couldn't help wondering if Megan would grow to look like her mother in later life.

'I'm afraid the Doctor's sedated her,' she said in her heavy Welsh accent, 'so you won't be able to speak to her.'

'Sedated?' echoed Jack, 'I hadn't realised it was that serious, I thought she'd just fainted.'

Encouraged by his concern she invited him in for a cup of tea. He could see that she was obviously distraught as she hurried around the kitchen nervously, nudging this, inconsequentially shifting that. Finally, after a long, strained silence, she turned to face him.

'She wouldn't go into her bedroom until we stripped off the wallpaper see, so she's asleep in the spare room.'

Jack was confused, 'Why is there a problem with the wallpaper?'

'Well, there was something about the pattern that upset her terribly and she kept going on about evil faces in it. Can't understand it, Dad and I picked it special see. We've never had this problem before,' she paused, obviously having difficulty relating the story. She leaned forward and placed a shaking hand on Jack's arm.

'Do you believe in demons?' she whispered.

Jack's mouth dropped open and he shook his head slowly, 'No! May I have a look at her room please?' he said on impulse.

'Well I don't know, do you think it might be haunted?'

The comment left Jack flustered, *is it possible?* He didn't know, but if her problem could be traced to her entering the portal, there may be some clues in her bedroom. Seeing that she was still expecting an answer, Jack said reassuringly, 'No of course not.'

Megan's father was busy stripping off the wallpaper crouched in a corner of the room, scraper in one hand wet paper in the other. He turned as Jack entered.

'What do you want, come to cause more trouble?' he grunted.

He levered himself into a slouch against the window sill and peered closely at Jack.

Jack felt intimidated; this was an enormous man, sprouting straggly hair like a huge fur ball. His piggy eyes were prominent within the fleshy face which seemed to be contorted into a permanent snarl. His whole manner was aggressive and threatening. It was common knowledge in the area that he had criminal connections, which seemed to provide his income, and a prison record for violent assault.

'How is she?' Jack inquired diplomatically.

'No better for seeing you,' growled the disgruntled giant, 'what did you do to her?'

'Nothing that I know of, I just happened to be around when she fainted,' Jack explained.

'It seems to me,' rumbled Megan's father, 'that you always "just happen to be around" when she's in trouble. So what do you want?'

Jack picked up a piece of the shredded wallpaper, 'Do you mind if I take this?' he said.

'Take the whole bloody lot, in fact you can strip it off the wall if you like,' he spat out.

Jack made a hasty retreat and was about to leave when Megan appeared in the hallway looking tired and frightened. He hastily stuffed the wallpaper into his pocket.

'I want to speak to you,' she said, and motioned him into the lounge. Megan's mother, with a wink and a smile, disappeared upstairs to help her husband.

'What happened? Your mother said something about demons,' he said incredulously.

Megan, through the occasional sob, managed to relate the happenings of the morning, ending with how she had fled from her room screaming hysterically.

'Where was I before I fainted?' she said suddenly, looking him straight in the eye. Jack was caught completely off guard.

'When?'

'Yesterday.'

'In the garden of a house, I carried you to the road.'

'How did you know?' she persisted.

'How did I know what?'

'That I was in the garden, chump.'

'I saw you go in there,' he lied.

She looked at him quizzically, remembering their previous conversation where he had agreed that she was behind him when she fainted. Feeling confused and frightened, she decided not to pursue the contradiction.

'Do you think I'm going mad Jack?'

'No of course not.'

'So you think it really happened?'

'Something must have happened to get you into this state,' he said.

'Jack, I'm afraid,' she said, clutching his arm.

Awkwardly, he briefly held her to him. She made to snuggle against him but he quickly released her.

'What did the doctor say?'

'Rest and take sleeping tablets,' she said mournfully.

'Give it a try over the weekend.'

Megan looked up at him appealingly, 'You'll come back and see me Jack?' she said.

'I'll try,' he replied.

CHAPTER 8

AS HE WALKED to Lucy's house he turned these events over in his mind and resolved to ask Lucy if there was anything that could be done about it. *After all*, he thought to himself, *the portal may be responsible for Megan's condition.*

Lucy watched him approaching from the upstairs window. *He's quite tall*, she thought, *and handsome in his juvenile way. Even though he doesn't know very much about the situation I've forced him into, he's stayed remarkably solid and dependable.* 'Yes,' she said to herself, 'I think I've chosen well, and he's cute too.'

She swung around and greeted him with a big smile as he entered the room.

'Is it alright?' he said pointing to the laptop.

'Exactly what I need, thank you Jack,' she said, beaming. 'Now, I think you deserve some explanations.'

'Tell me about your father,' he interjected.

'Oh yes,' she said, 'he was deported for spying.'

'Was he?'

'Was he what?'

'A spy?'

'No of course not,' she snapped, 'but yes he was deported, in fact we both were. The Foreign Office became very nervous when they realised what we were doing in our research and needed an excuse to terminate his stay at the university without attracting too much attention to the nature of his work.'

'So why did they have a problem with your research?' he asked.

'I don't think you've realised yet the possible consequences of this,' she waved a hand at the computer, 'if we can get this working over large distances, it will cause massive changes in the way the world is organised.'

'How do you mean?'

'What's the single most important commodity in the world, the thing that the whole world relies upon and around which the whole of industry is structured?'

Jack felt flustered, as though he was back in the classroom. 'Well, oil, I suppose,' he said hesitantly.

'Yes!'

Lucy rose from the chair and the whiff of carbolic drifted across to Jack as she lifted her arms in dramatic fashion, palms outstretched towards him.

'So if you didn't need oil for transport?'

'The oil industry would almost be redundant?' said Jack.

'Yes, and guess who would be interested in stopping this research if they knew it existed? People with a large investment in the oil industry who would stand to lose their fortunes almost overnight. Of course they would fight it! And they *are* powerful people.'

'What would they do if they knew?'

'Who knows if they would even stop short at assassination? It would be done quietly of course, without attracting attention.'

Jack shuddered as he realised the frightening possibility of been hunted down by the oil industry.

'Why did you stay?'

'I had no choice if we were to continue our experiments. We had to construct another portal far away to prove that we could transport between them. The Government helped us there by deporting my father.'

'Really!' said Jack, his eyes wide with amazement, 'And can you?'

'Not yet, but we are close. Father is making good progress in China.'

He gave a low whistle, 'I can see why the F.O. got the willies about this. If it works, you could transport a whole army in secrecy almost anywhere you could construct a portal.'

'Exactly!' she said.

'You realise how dangerous this is, but you still continue to do it?'

'Yes,' she said, 'but we're not going to stop progress just because governments get nervous, are we? If science had been reluctant to rock the political boat in the past we would still be cave dwellers.'

Jack sighed resignedly, 'Well I suppose so, but don't you think this should be regulated by some authority?'

'Pah!' she spat out, 'If you allowed the authorities in on this they would stifle it out of existence with red tape and the pressure exerted by vested interests.'

'Oh why did I ever get mixed up in this?' he groaned, 'I'm just a simple "A" level student hoping to pass his exams and have a pretty unspectacular life after that. Maybe go to university, get drunk fairly frequently, with the occasional orgy. It was never my ambition to be the most wanted man in England.'

'Some of us just get lucky,' she said with a wry grin. 'Look at it this way; you're involved in a major scientific advance which will bring fantastic benefits for mankind, and yourself.'

'If I stay out of jail long enough,' he said morosely.

'I'll level with you now Jack, the reason the computer was switched off the other day was because the police came snooping around looking for me, they switched it off and left me stranded.'

'The police! Ah! Now I see why you said you don't exist. So you're hunted by the police, but why would they be looking for you if they thought you were in China?'

'Because they know I'm not. Thanks to my father's laptop I disappeared into the other dimension at the airport, and left a duplicate of myself behind. It was the duplicate the police saw going into the departure lounge, not me! Father got rid of it before boarding the plane. Unfortunately the police switched off my computer at home leaving me stranded. They know I didn't get off the 'plane in China, so they assume I'm still here.'

'Are the police watching this house?'

'They were; which is why I didn't want you to switch on any lights. No, they've been told to stop, but that won't be the end of it. There are other government departments who are still keenly interested.'

'When did all this happen, I mean the deportation and all that?'

'Last Monday; why?'

'So where are you sleeping and eating?'

'I don't see why you should be interested in my domestic arrangements,' she said coyly, 'but for two days I was stuck in another dimension, until you came along.'

'So why are the police happy to leave the computer in the house?' he said, changing the subject.

Lucy frowned, 'Now that's the thing that I can't understand. I must admit I'm very uneasy about that and that's why I need this.' she said patting the laptop computer. 'This should allow me to construct a portal anywhere I please as long as you're around to look after me.' This was accompanied with a coquettish come hither look which made Jack's knees go weak.

Embarrassed, he stuttered, 'I . . . I . . . see, but can't the police figure out what's going on by examining this?' he pointed at the desktop computer.

'No, to them it will appear to be an ordinary computer, only when you put this in,' she waved the DVD, 'and type in the password, does it become a quantum computer.'

She was interrupted by a soft click from the computer and turning to it accessed the email, 'This will be my father,' she said.

A round faced, grey bearded Chinaman appeared on the computer screen. He was not at all how Jack had imagined him. His eyes twinkled as he smiled at his daughter, crinkling the laughter lines around them. His firm jaw and full, determined mouth suggested that he was used to being obeyed. He was effusive with his greeting of Lucy as was she with him. For a while Jack felt inadequate, like an intruder at a private family party. He contented himself by reflecting on the situation he found himself in. Suddenly the conversation was in English and directed at him.

'My name Chu,' he said in broken English, 'please to meet you Jack. Are you taking care of my little girl?'

'Well . . . , yes,' said Jack suddenly confused, 'I suppose so.'

'This project very important for future; civilisation may depend upon it, you understand Jack?'

He was completely overwhelmed by that thought and could only stammer in response, 'I'll do my best to help.'

'Lucy told me you good boy, that OK for me,' he said.

There was more conversation with Lucy in Chinese and then he was gone.

"This project very important for future, civilisation may depend upon it." The words had a remarkable effect on Jack. Here was something worthwhile which only he could do. Others were dependent upon him and he had responsibilities He was suddenly infused with a sense of pride. Lucy was right, he couldn't refuse this opportunity. He had warmed to her father in a way he could not to his own. The obstacles, hardships and frustrations to be endured, seemed insignificant when set against the potential benefits for the whole of mankind. He had to be part of it!

For a while Lucy was restrained and quiet after the conversation with her father. Jack gave her some time to recover herself then introduced the subject that was causing him some concern.

'Megan's not very well,' he ventured.

'Pah! Silly girl, she shouldn't be interfering in other people's business. Are you sure she can't remember anything?'

'Quite sure,' he said emphatically, 'but I do think she may need some help.'

He repeated the conversation he had had with her earlier. Lucy's dark brown eyes became momentarily clouded with doubt, and then as if deliberately dismissing any empathy she sprang to her feet exclaiming, 'I'm not interested in your girl friend's problems. She is your problem, not mine!'

Jack was taken aback by the vehemence with which this was delivered but recovered quickly saying equally forcefully, 'I think if you caused her problem, you ought to help her solve it.'

Lucy's eyes flashed angrily, 'I have important work, I can't afford to spend time holding a little girl's hand,' she cried.

He could see he was not going to convince her, so with a curt goodbye; he ran down the stairs and left the house muttering to himself angrily, 'She'll have to come around in the end.'

He spent a troubled morning at home with the problem running around in his head. What made things worse was that his mother had been to Megan's house in his absence and had winkled the whole story out of her mother. Now she was armed with a barrage of questions. Jack managed to fend off most of them without arousing too much suspicion and finally escaped to his bedroom where he could think in peace.

Although excited, he felt overwhelmed by it all when he was not with Lucy. Teleportation, spies, haunted rooms, oil industry; this was like something you watched on television, it didn't happen in real life did it? Well not to a seventeen year old boy with no experience of these things. That was a worry, but what was worse he had to keep it all a secret. He still had nagging doubts about the motivation of Lucy and her father. *Don't be stupid,* he scolded himself, *a more unlikely pair of candidates for the role of world domination I couldn't imagine, a wizened old professor and his teenage daughter.* No! They, like himself, were the victims of circumstances and needed all the help they could get to stay out of trouble. Juvenile thoughts of heroic deeds flitted through his mind for a while and then were swiftly dismissed. This was not something requiring a heroic deed mentality, he reasoned; it was far too subtle for that.

Where did she go when she broke free from her body? Wherever it was she could still communicate with the boring old third dimension, and reorganise other people's computers to suit herself. *Now there's a thought,* he mused and switched on his own computer. It had occurred to him that he could do some research on his own account, in a small way, by reading some "A" level notes which he had on the subject of quantum mechanics.

As he started his computer, he noticed he had received an email. It was from Lucy, 'Sorry I didn't mean to upset you, I've thought about the problem and you're right, I should investigate. See you about six pm?' He quickly replied to her request and then returned to his own investigations.

By mid afternoon, Jack felt more like his old self as he made his way back to the school. The low angry clouds and bitter wind did nothing to dispel his enthusiasm as he looked forward to the afternoon football match against a rival school. Dipper greeted him as he swung through the school gate.

'What are you doing here?' exclaimed Jack, 'I thought you hated football.'

'I do, I just like to see you make a fool of yourself,' he said, pulling his woolly hat more firmly down onto his round head. This gave him the appearance of a startled owl. Jack chuckled, 'And you think I look foolish?' he countered.

The swirling wind made the quality of play difficult but even that could not explain the extraordinary happenings of the second half. It had looked as though Dipper's assessment of Jack's performance was correct in the first period of play. Everything he attempted went wrong. In his position at central defence, this resulted in a three goal deficit. The rest of the team shunned Jack as they chewed on stringy oranges at half time. Dipper sidled up to him.

'Look,' he started, 'I don't know much about football, but . . . .'

'You're right.' growled Jack.

The second half got under way with an immediate goal from Jack's team and an increase in their determination. The opposition had other ideas however and he was kept busy for a while in his own penalty area, until a harmless cross ball floated to him which he carelessly punted down the field. A gust of wind lifted the ball and carried it to the opposite penalty area. The ball dropped gently towards the goalkeeper who waited with outstretched arms to catch it. The ball suddenly gathered speed and made a sharp detour around the goalkeeper finally rolling over the goal line. There was a stunned silence from both teams for an instant and then Jack was mobbed by his team-mates. He was still considering this unlikely event as his team forced a corner and he trotted forward into the opposition penalty area. The corner was taken and the ball swung into the goalkeeper who punched it forcibly out straight onto Jack's head. He fell as if pole axed, the ball hammered into the crossbar and once again flew out, bounced off his prone body and dropped in a large arc towards the goal. A defender jumped to head the ball away, but as he was about to make contact it swerved around his head and flew into the goal. Once again Jack was credited with the unlikely goal. His team were by now well and truly determined to make this a victory despite the nature of the dramatic turnaround in fortune. Jack, however, was beginning to get suspicious and decided to check out his feeling that all was not above board. The opportunity arose near the end of the game with the teams still drawing at three goals each. The ball came to Jack on the edge of his own penalty area, so he turned and tapped it back to his goalkeeper. It trickled along the ground and stopped in a muddy puddle. The goalkeeper swung a boot at it whereupon the ball avoided his kick by swerving. Picking up speed it began to roll along the ground pursued by the frantic goalkeeper, who attempted to stop it by placing his foot on it. It wriggled out from under his foot and squirted across the goal line. The opposition were helpless with mirth at this fiasco, while Jack, his fears confirmed, was getting angry. Shortly afterwards the final whistle blew and he and his disconsolate team trudged back to the dressing room. As they changed, conversation was mainly restricted to expletives directed at him. He hurried out before too many serious questions were asked. Dipper was waiting outside for him and fell in alongside as they walked out of the school gate.

'Now I'm the first to admit,' he began, 'that my knowledge of football is very limited, however even I think it's not a good idea to score in your own goal.'

'It was blown by the wind,' grunted Jack, hoping he wouldn't pursue it further.

'It looked a bit unlikely to me; the ball seemed to have a life of its own.' Dipper peered at him waiting for some reaction as they continued down the road.

There was none. *Let him think what he wants*, thought Jack, *nobody can prove anything and the incident will blow over in time*.

'Looked very odd to me, I mean, a ball doing its own thing like,' ventured Dipper again.

'What are you doing the rest of the day?' said Jack deliberately changing the subject, and hoping to throw him off course.

'Homework,' he groaned, 'you can be sure there's always that to do. Then I thought I might go down to the club and have a game of snooker, see if I can use some of the variations on Newton's laws of motion I've learned this afternoon.'

Oh! flip, thought Jack as they parted, *he's not going to let this go. Once he's got his teeth into something he won't give up, that's his nature.*

He remembered how, when Smithy had an aberration and had miscalculated a formula. Not wanting to lose face in front of the class, Smithy had brushed aside Dipper's immediate objection. For Dipper this became the mathematical equivalent of the Holy Grail, and he immersed himself in the subject until he was more conversant with the minutiae than Smithy. A battle of wills ensued resulting in denial on Smithy's part and an interview with the Headmaster on Dipper's. Dipper stopped short of wringing an apology from Smithy, but everybody in the sixth form was aware of the result and applauded his persistence. *Dipper, when roused, could be difficult to contain*, thought Jack.

CHAPTER 9

THE POTENTIAL THREAT posed by Dipper's curiosity was discussed when he spoke to Lucy later that evening.

He stumbled on the stairs in the dark and accidentally dislodged a ceremonial sword from the wall sending it clattering to the bottom.

'You'd never sneak up on anybody would you? Is there a problem?' she said, noting the serious look on his face.

'You could say that,' he retorted frostily.

She quickly fastened onto the cause of his concern, 'It's the football match isn't it?'

'Mm!' he grunted in faint surprise, 'Why did you have to interfere?'

'I didn't,' she replied.

'Oh, I suppose it was the hand of God.'

'No! It was Crip.'

He slumped on the edge of her desk, an incredulous expression on his face and spread his hands in exasperation.

'Why?'

'He thought he was trying to help you, he likes to help.'

'Where is he? I want to staple him to the floor,' growled Jack.

'Don't be too hard on him,' she said appealingly.

'You don't understand, he's roused the best bloodhound in the sixth form. He won't rest until he finds an answer.'

'You mean your friend, what do you call him Dipper?'

'Yes, he'll keep shaking it until something falls out.'

'Mm!' said Lucy thoughtfully, 'Strange name, "Dipper".'

'It's a nickname; his real name is Brian . . . Brian Tubb.'

'So how did he become Dipper?'

'Brian Tubb . . . bran tub . . . lucky dip . . . Dipper, see?'

Lucy looked puzzled.

'Bran tub, lucky dip?' he repeated hopefully.

Lucy's puzzled frown deepened.

'Never mind, it's not important.'

'Don't worry,' she said, 'I'll deal with Dipper. Some auto suggestion should do the trick.'

Jack looked doubtful. From what he'd seen of this remarkable girl so far he thought she was probably capable of a lot, but controlling Dipper's inquisitive nature full time? Maybe she could, then again maybe she couldn't.

'I think it may be a good idea to add the rules of football into Crip's forty thousand pages,' he said, 'along with an instruction to help only when asked.'

'Point taken,' she said as though suddenly bored with the subject. Her mind was busy with more important matters. She rose from the desk and motioned him to sit down. As he did so the smell of carbolic wafted into his nostrils and he couldn't resist making a comment.

'Nice perfume.'

She laughed, 'There's tons of the stuff upstairs, Father thought it was the best thing invented in England, so he bought a job lot.'

'What is it? It smells like a hospital.'

'Soap,' she replied, 'carbolic soap, or Phenol to give it its correct title. It was invented by someone called Lister in the nineteenth century, as an antiseptic for treating amputees.'

He flinched at the thought of medical things, 'What did your father use it for?' he said bracing himself for a bizarre reply.

Lucy's eyes twinkled in delight, 'Washing! What else?' she laughed.

'He doesn't like England much then?'

'Best of the worst, I think he would say.'

'And what do you think?'

'I am English,' she said haughtily, 'I was born here, in London.'

'So what about your mother, you weren't a by-product of a computer programme were you?'

She ignored his sarcasm and drew a deep breath as if preparing a well rehearsed speech, 'My mother is Italian,' she began.

'What a mixture,' he exclaimed in surprise.

Lucy gave him a cold look, rocking on her heels for a moment.

'My mother is Italian,' she repeated and paused, 'she is employed by "E.N.I.", in Rotterdam.'

'What's "E.N.I."?'

'It's an Italian oil company; she is a Senior Marketing Executive.'

'So don't they mind being separated?'

'They have different careers,' she responded sharply.

He detected that this was a subject best left alone but his curiosity was mounting, Italian mother working in Holland for a major oil company, Chinese father working on a project which could threaten the nature of the oil industry. Still, he thought, an Italian mother could explain her occasional fiery outbursts which, as far as he knew, were not normally a characteristic of Chinese girls. The next question was on the tip of his tongue, but Lucy, as if anticipating its nature cut across his thoughts.

'OK,' she said brusquely, 'let's find what's troubling Megan.'

She left him with the necessary instructions and went down to the conservatory but couldn't resist throwing a teasing remark over her shoulder as she left, 'I'll find what's troubling your girlfriend.'

Taking the bait, he protested, 'She's not my girlfriend,' but Lucy had gone, leaving only a mischievous chuckle behind. Within five minutes of entering the portal, she had returned.

'Well?' said Jack rising from the desk.

'There seems to be some interest in our activity,' she said cautiously.

'What does that mean?' he inquired, impatiently pacing back and forth. 'Where do you go anyway, and how does this affect Megan?'

'OK I'll tell you, you've been very patient and you deserve some sort of explanation,' she said, as she sat down.

'As you've already seen, when I enter the other dimension, I lose my physical part, my body. Everything is thought there, or what some people call spirit or pure energy without form.'

'Is this what we call the astral plane?' interrupted Jack.

'It's not a good idea to attach second hand titles to it,' she responded guardedly and continued, 'the entities which exist there are broadly two types, those which need to rise to higher levels of existence and those who still want the pleasures of the physical world. Of course this situation already exists in the third dimension. The people alive now will simply continue their tendencies over into the other dimensions.'

'You mean people who have died?' he cried, becoming alarmed.

'Yes,' she said, 'the ones who continue to desire a physical existence are usually the mischievous ones who break through into our dimension and cause disturbances by using people as a medium for their expression.'

'And this is what has affected Megan?'

'Difficult to tell, it may be that she's been spotted as a means of entering our dimension, it really depends upon how susceptible she is.'

'Let me get this straight in my head,' said Jack, 'Megan appeared for a few minutes in some other dimension and could have been seen as a means of entering our dimension by a dead person wanting to become physical again?'

'That's it in a nutshell.'

'So why don't dead people target you?'

'I take precautions,' replied Lucy.

He was having difficulty in coming to terms with these latest revelations. She was about to continue but he interrupted her, 'So if these undesirable people seeking a physical existence were to discover your portal, and how to reverse your process, they could populate our dimension? You could have hordes of previously dead people, with nothing to lose, invading the planet looking for physical gratification.'

She was temporarily stunned into silence as she understood the implications of Jack's statement. Her small hands pulled a hank of long black hair over her shoulder and began to twiddle with it nervously. This was the first time Jack had seen her in doubt about anything and it disturbed him. Maybe she wasn't infallible after all!

'Well I suppose it's possible,' she said finally.

The resulting strained silence was broken by Jack, 'Well, what are you going to do about it, Einstein?' he said sarcastically.

'I'll talk to Father,' she said quietly.

Tears were welling in the corners of her almond shaped eyes. Regretting his careless remark he moved to comfort her, 'I'm sorry,' he said, 'that was unkind,' but she shrugged him away, her eyes once more blazing defiantly.

'I will talk to my father, now please leave me,' she said tersely.

CHAPTER 10

WHEN JACK GOT home his parents were lying in wait for him. They wanted to know his intentions towards his career and they were clearly not going to give up until they were satisfied. He sat down wearily, aware that there was nowhere to hide, and resolved to see it through.

'But Dad,' he said, 'you knew when I decided to do the sciences that I wasn't intending to go in for a career in Law.'

'I thought it was just a fad,' said Nigel waving a careless arm, 'besides everything's arranged for you, when you've finished at law school there's a place for you in the firm, only a junior position to begin with, but you'll soon rise through the ranks.'

His mother nodded her assent, 'It's a good career son, look how well your father's done.'

'Look Dad, I am grateful for what you're trying to do for me, but you wouldn't want me to be unhappy doing something I didn't like, would you?'

Nigel, shaking with anger, rose from his chair and glared up at Jack. 'That's really the problem isn't it; being happy is the only thing that matters to you?' Betty quickly moved to defuse the situation and laid a restraining hand on Nigel's arm.

'Now then, let's not get into an argument over this,' she said smoothly.

Jack looked around the room at the lifestyle he was been encouraged to emulate then despairingly at the mantle clock steadily draining their life away. He fought back the disparaging comment that was on the tip of his tongue and became yet more determined to do something exciting with his life. His experiences of the last few days had revealed possibilities previously undreamed of, and he wasn't about to trade that in for the boring life of an articled clerk.

'Well I'm going to finish my "A" levels whatever,' he sighed, 'and we'll see after that.'

Nigel gave his wife a meaningful glance, but Betty knew the matter was far from resolved. The phone rang and she hurried into the hall to answer it. 'It's for you Jack, I think it's Megan,' she said, with a knowing look at Nigel.

Normally Jack would not have arranged a date with Megan under any circumstances but when she suggested they go to McDonald's for a snack because she wanted to talk with him, he gladly took the excuse to escape from his parents' grilling.

Nigel and Betty realising they could not pursue the conversation further returned to their sedentary occupations. The mantle clock ticked steadily on.

. . . .

Jack sat on Megan's bed and surveyed the new wallpaper with some alarm, 'Stripes!' he cried, 'Up and down stripes, what were they thinking of, they've turned it into a prison cell.'

'It's better than the lunatic asylum I had before,' she replied as she combed her hair at her small dressing table.

He glanced at the book on her bedside table, 'What are you reading?'

'Oh it's just an art book,' she said, threading her pony tail through an elastic band.

'I didn't know you were interested in art.'

He picked up the book and flicked through the pages as he waited for Megan to finish getting ready. 'Ugh!' he said, 'This is gruesome, who painted this?'

She glanced over his shoulder, 'Oh they're paintings by Hieronymous Bosch, cute aren't they?'

'They're awful,' he said, 'all these scenes of sadistic torture with freakish little devils running around. No wonder you're having nightmares. When were these done?'

'Fifteenth century I think. Come on; I'm ready.'

There was no queue at McDonald's. Jack collected two double beef burgers and chips while Megan went to the toilet. He took the loaded tray over to a table and sat down wondering why Megan wanted to speak to him. He was idly sucking on a chip, gazing into the distance when his eyes suddenly focused as a familiar voice broke through his reverie; 'Why thanks Jack, how did you know I was going to be coming in here, I see I'm not the only one who's psychic, Mm! Beef burger! This is just what I need, I'm starving.'

He choked on the chip he had in his mouth, but before he could say anything Lucy launched excitedly into an explanation of her conversation with her father. Panic seized him and he froze as Megan appeared behind Lucy wearing an incredulous expression. She quickly recovered from her astonishment whipped the plate from under his nose and sat down. He knew he couldn't give Megan a plausible explanation, his mind had gone numb anyway and his throat had constricted in a tight knot.

Lucy stopped speaking as Megan seated herself. For what seemed an age to Jack, the three of them sat in stony silence. Finally Megan broke the impasse, 'Aren't you going to introduce me to your Oriental friend Jack?' she said provocatively.

The McDonald's counter staff had by now sensed that when Jack appeared there was likely to be entertainment and stopped their normal activities to observe the action.

Jack stammered, 'This is Lucy, she is . . . ,'

Lucy beamed and finished his sentence, '. . . his girlfriend.'

Megan was stunned and looked at him, waiting for confirmation. He spread his hands in a helpless gesture and was about to speak, but she had heard enough. Picking up a tomato sauce bottle she deliberately unscrewed the top then upended the contents over Jack's head. Sobbing, she ran out into the street.

McDonald's rocked to the sound of the counter staff's raucous laughter. Ketchup slowly matted his hair and crept down his nose as Lucy whooped in delight.

'You do look a sight,' she laughed, 'and there's more food left for me.'

He dragged an inadequate paper napkin across his face in an effort to stem the slowly descending red tide.

'Why did you say that?' he said through clenched teeth.

'Oh I'm so sorry,' she said with mock humility, 'did I spoil your lover's tryst? You don't want to be wasting your time with her; there are more exciting things to be doing.'

'That's not the point,' he said, flicking a blob of ketchup at her, 'I think she was going to tell me some more about her hallucinations; it could have been useful.'

Lucy was suddenly serious, 'Oh! I'm sorry, I thought you two were . . . you know . . .'

'No! For once your information was wrong, Lucy witch.'

She smiled sweetly at him, 'Oh dear, I've been an idiot haven't I? You really are working with me on this now aren't you?'

'Yes, well, I had a conversation with my parents earlier which could have caused me to have a career climbing mountains rather than do what they wanted.'

'Oh I see, so my little interest is a sort of, diversion, an escape for you is it?'

She had a half smile on her face and her eyes were dancing as she teased him. Jack was in no mood for her *come hither* antics and made to leave the table.

'Hold on,' she said, 'only joking; anyway you haven't heard all my news yet.'

'Go on,' he said, becoming aware of several pairs of eyes curiously watching them in eager anticipation, 'and hurry up I have to go home and get a shower.'

'Don't worry darling,' she teased, 'you look just as lovely as ever, even with red hair.' Jack made to rise again from the table.

'Ok, I'll behave. I spoke with my father and he was already aware of the possibility you suggested. He's done a lot of work on the problem and is well advanced with a solution.'

'When?'

'When what?' retorted Lucy.

'When will he have a solution?'

'Maybe in a few months.'

'Maybe too late.'

'You are a very irritating boyfriend,' cried Lucy.

'But this time very right,' he insisted.

. . . .

Sunday afternoons had been like this as long as he could remember. It was as though real life had been suspended until the following day. He glanced at his father who was slumped in his chair dozing. The steady droning of his shallow breathing was punctuated with the clack-clack of knitting needles beating a regular rhythm as Betty absentmindedly pursued her favourite pastime. He shifted uncomfortably in his chair. The mantle clock ticked on remorselessly. He noted the time and with some satisfaction realised that Dipper would arrive shortly, he was always punctual.

With considerable relief Jack jumped to his feet as Dipper's plump shape flitted past the lounge window.

'Am I glad to see you,' he said as they headed upstairs to Jack's room, 'I thought I was going to die and nobody would notice.'

'Sundays are a bit tedious,' agreed Dipper, flopping on Jack's bed which creaked alarmingly in response.

'So cheer me up,' said Jack despondently.

'Don't see your problem,' said Dipper, 'you're a young chap; whole exciting life stretching out in front of you; plenty of interesting challenges to keep you motivated; where's the problem?'

'You've been talking to the careers people again haven't you?'

Dipper smiled, 'And you've had a sense of humour failure.'

Jack sighed and slumped into the bedside chair. 'It's all getting very complicated,' he began.

'Mm!' Dipper interrupted, 'And you can't tell me about it.'

Jack was momentarily startled by this apparent insight, *maybe it's just probing on his part, you never can tell with Dipper*, he thought.

Noting his discomfort and being anxious to help his friend, Dipper levered himself off the bed and strode purposefully to the window. He jammed his hands firmly in his pockets and gazed out onto the street lit by a watery sun.

'If this is about your parents and their plans for you, remember it's your life, I mean in the end you're stuck with whatever you decide. So just decide, then apologise to everybody and get on with it.' He turned on his heel and looked at Jack judging the impact of his statement.

'You're absolutely right. Sod 'em,' said Jack forcefully, with more confidence than he really felt. 'What do *you* want to do?'

Dipper turned once more to the window and paused before replying, 'Media.'

Jack was surprised by the abruptness of the response, 'Doing what?' he said.

'I want to expose hypocrisy and corruption in high places.'

'Oh!' breathed Jack, 'I never realised you had such high moral ambitions.'

'No!' said Dipper turning again and spreading his chubby hands, 'Don't be fooled by appearances, I could become the biggest pain in the arse for this country's establishment.'

This was said with such conviction and more than a hint of bitterness that a chill ran down Jack's spine. 'That's going to make little money but plenty of enemies,' he said.

'Money's the problem, not the solution.'

As they were talking, Jack's computer flickered into life. Crip appeared on the screen and tapped the inside of it with a dull clinking sound while looking appealingly at Jack, inevitably arousing Dipper's interest.

'What's that?' he said pointing at the screen. 'Haven't I seen that somewhere before?'

Jack hastily reached over to the computer and minimised it, 'Oh! Just something I downloaded from the internet.'

Dipper screwed up his nose and his eyes became even more prominent behind the bottle-glass. 'There have been some very odd things happening around here lately and you have been behaving strangely. I'm beginning to connect the two; is there anything you want to tell me?'

'No, I think you're letting your imagination run away with you.'

'Maybe,' he said doubtfully.

Jack hastily changed the subject, 'I don't understand why you're doing "A" level physics if you have ambitions to be a media tycoon.'

'I suppose you'd expect me to do history, economics, something like that?'

Jack nodded, desperately hoping he had been deflected. Dipper ambled across to the bed and once more strained its resilience.

'For me it's about the future or the past. Economics and history are concerned to a large degree with what's happened, which I don't deny is very useful, but science is the future. More than anything science will determine the course of human events, and I want to be part of shaping that future. So you see I have to understand it, in order to comment on it.'

Jack considered how different he and his friend were. In spite of his obvious physical shortcomings he was determined and resolute, or was that because of them? He was mentally very strong and Jack found himself admiring and envying those attributes while underestimating his own.

'Do you think big business holds back innovation?'

'Certainly if it's in their interests to do it,' replied Dipper.

'So if say, someone invented a way of using water as a fuel, the oil industry would resist it?'

'I would think so. Just think of the upheaval that would create. It would be an overnight disaster for the world economy. I would think they would certainly resist, for however long it took them to find a way to turn it to their advantage and profit from it.'

'I remember Smithy telling us about the everlasting light bulb,' said Jack, 'how it was invented at the beginning of last century and then was dumped in order to maintain the light bulb industry.'

'Yes, that's a good example of killing innovation by commercial interest,' agreed Dipper.

Both young men lapsed into silence for a few minutes, Dipper finally changing the subject with, 'So how's the love life going with Megan?'

'You know there's nothing going on there,' protested Jack.

'Jack, old chap, we're friends, you know you can tell me everything,' teased Dipper with a broad grin, 'get it off your chest you'll feel so much better for it.'

Jack jumped out of his chair and levered him off the bed. He flopped on the floor with a tremendous thump causing Nigel to awake downstairs with a start. Raucous laughter echoed around the house as downstairs, Nigel struggled to his feet and headed for the hall.

'If you're going to fight, do it outside!' he yelled up the stairs.

'Come on let's go for a walk,' said Jack giving Dipper a cursory kick on his ample buttocks, 'don't want to disturb the hospice.'

. . . .

Jack never liked Monday mornings but this one was worse than usual. As he started out to school he was filled with apprehension, for although the fiasco at McDonald's was not of his making, he knew Megan would not see it that way. He was also afraid that Megan may gossip about Lucy at school. He need not have worried on that score for her pride would not allow her to discuss with anyone else the embarrassment she had suffered. He was relieved to see that she did not intercept him on the way to school. Nevertheless he was still concerned for her safety and was upset when she deliberately ignored him in class later that morning.

For her part Megan was feeling strangely calm. She realised that Jack had in no way committed himself to her, so why should he not have a girlfriend? She was however intrigued by this mysterious girl who had apparently suddenly appeared in Jack's life. Why had he not told her about this girl, and why had he invited her to McDonald's when he knew she, Megan, wanted to talk with him in private? She suddenly remembered the voice in the headphones, which had been rude to her on the way home from school. It could be the same voice she thought.

Unusually, she was not paying attention in class but it went unnoticed by Smithy who, with chin resting on the palm of one hand while his elbow rested on the desk, read aloud from his exercise book. Jack was sitting behind Megan and wondering how Smithy still managed to use his ancient notes in an ever changing scientific world and why he needed the book anyway. *After all,* he reasoned, *he should know it off by heart by now.* To all outward appearances the only thing about him which suggested he wasn't asleep was his lips moving and the thin reedy monotone coming from them.

A rubber band looped lazily across the classroom and landed on Megan's head. She made no move to brush it away but remained deep in thought. The empty desk in front of her began to rise unaided until it hovered a half metre above the floor.

Smithy glanced up from his notes sensing that something was conscious in his classroom other than himself. On spotting the elevated desk he remarked laconically, 'I would like to point out to whoever is playing the fool with that desk, that this is a theoretical physics lesson, not a practical one.' Heads turned to look at the desk and there were some stifled sniggers. Megan remained motionless, oblivious to the object of their mirth. The desk, as if offended, shook violently and threw itself out of the window. There was a stunned silence as the sound of shattering glass and wood subsided. Jack's chair developed an alarming list and he was dumped on the floor, whereupon the classroom erupted into mayhem, while its occupants scrambled for the door. Desks, chairs, bags and books flew around the room as if in a maelstrom. Throughout, Megan remained strangely calm in contrast to the scenes of utter chaos going on around her and made her way to the door along with her classmates.

As all assembled outside the tension gave way to relieved laughter and the furore inside the classroom subsided as quickly as it had begun. Smithy was absolutely distraught, his precious exercise book being dealt a mortal blow by a flying chair leg. 'Good antigravity demo sir,' somebody shouted after him as he fled down the corridor to report the incident, 'must have been a poltergeist.'

Dipper grabbed Jack by the elbow, 'Did you see that?' he said excitedly.

'I was in the middle of it, you twerp, of course I saw it.'

'No! Not that! I mean Megan.'

Jack began to feel uncomfortable again; Dipper seemed to be having that effect on him lately.

'She looked as if she was in a trance,' he continued, 'it happens like that in films. I think she's been possessed.'

Ouch! thought Jack, *He could be right.* 'Oh no, I think she was just dazed by the whole thing,' he said.

'Mm, maybe,' said Dipper doubtfully.

. . . .

Collins surveyed the wreck of the classroom. Sweat was standing out on his forehead despite the icy blast funnelling through the broken window. The portly caretaker watched him carefully, trying to anticipate his reaction.

'I'll need to take statements from some of the pupils and the teacher, what's his name, Mr Smith?' said Collins officiously.

The caretaker tilted his head into a vigorous ear poke, as if removing an obstruction, 'Kids won't be a problem mate, they'll love it, but Mr Smiff went orf sick an' we don't know when 'e'll be coming back, if ever. See, 'is exercise book was ruined an' you can't do much for a teacher when 'is exercise book's been wrecked. It's a bit like a security blanket. Take it away an' instant stress. 'E could be orf sick for six munfs or more. Terrible stressful you know mate, we may never see 'im again mate.' This was accompanied with semaphore like, jerky, hand movements as though he were directing traffic.

Collins frowned at this performance and picked his way through the broken furniture with the caretaker in close attendance.

'Story is, there wus one o' them poultrygest thingys,' he said. 'Didn't see it meself, I was too busy with me boilers.'

Collins spotted something on the floor and pulled on his thin latex gloves. He bent down and picked it up between finger and thumb.

'What the 'eck is that?' said the caretaker, peering at the object. Collins pushed it under his nose whereupon he screwed up his face in disgust, 'Pooh!'

'Exactly,' agreed Collins, 'did they keep pets in this room?'

'Not that I know of mate,' replied the caretaker, 'maybe one of the kids dropped one in fright.'

Collins gingerly fed the object into a plastic bag and sealed it.

. . . . — . . . .

Collins shifted anxiously in his chair as Livingstone leafed through the statements, dropping them carelessly on the desk one by one. This was something he had not been looking forward to, as he was acutely aware that they bordered on farce and melodrama in equal proportions provided, as they were, by a group of highly creative sixth formers. He had prepared some defence against the expected onslaught and was braced for the criticism about wasting police time. "Incidents like this should be dealt with by the school's own disciplinary system as it was clearly a case of vandalism by the pupils", was what he expected to hear from Livingstone.

His boss remained impassive until he finally dropped the last statement, leaned back in his chair, swung his legs up onto the desk and beamed at Collins, 'Well done lad, good statements, have you got the sample?'

Taken aback by this response, Collins fumbled for the plastic bag and pushed it across the desk.

'Is that what I think it is?' muttered Livingstone peering cautiously at the squashy mess through the protective plastic.

'I think so boss. It wasn't like that at first, more solid like, but it's been in my pocket and what with the heat and movement it seems to have got . . . ,

Yes! All right don't go on,' interrupted Livingstone hastily. 'You can forget all about this incident now. Forensic will deal with this and I'll take it from here,' he said with a smug beam.

CHAPTER 11

THE TEMPORARY PHYSICS teacher was a vast improvement on his predecessor and was installed, according to the rest of the staff, with unreasonable haste. In fact some people remarked that it was almost as though he was available too quickly. The feeling among the teachers was that he had replaced poor old Smithy before his exercise book was cold in its grave. Some girls in the class certainly approved of him and had approached him with fluttering eyelashes and the giggling entreaty, 'Will you be staying sir?'

He had a muscular physique, short blond hair slightly greying at the temples, good regular features with a strong jaw line and appealing air of self assurance. His piercing blue eyes missed nothing, but most misdemeanours were dealt with in a thoughtful manner. The boys soon realised he could be firm in a friendly, supportive way and on the whole respected him. Everybody noticed that the index finger of his left hand was missing, but this soon became old news and for the most part was ignored.

Mr White rapidly became known with some affection as *Chalky* and the class quickly settled down once more to the humdrum routines of school life.

Megan remained steadfastly unimpressed by Chalky. She was more concerned with her own worries and became increasingly restless. Finally consigning her hurt to history, she approached Jack in a break from lessons and poured out her fears.

'Jack, I think I caused that destruction in the classroom.'

'Well, we don't know what it was, we probably never will know,' he said uneasily, 'so don't go worrying about it.'

'What if it keeps happening and it's me that's causing it?'

'I'm sure it's not you, it was just a freak thing, it won't happen again,' he said, reassuringly.

He was secretly relieved that the incident in the classroom was temporarily occupying her mind and diverting her from asking awkward questions about Lucy. He decided he must think up some sort of story which would satisfy her curiosity on that score. Even so he began to be concerned himself, wondering if there was some truth in what she said and decided to talk to Lucy about it.

. . . .

Livingstone peered disbelievingly at the forensic report and turned it over several times to see if anything was written on the back, to no avail.

"Probably animal," he read, "but of no known species." What the hell are they talking about?' he muttered, reaching for the phone handset, which he predictably sent spinning upwards with a crash before catching it neatly. He stabbed out a number and twiddled his pencil, while his frown became a permanent scowl. The voice at the other end of the phone was obviously anticipating the call and was unapologetic.

'We've tested the D.N.A. and it has no correspondence whatever with any known animal, except we think it's the size of a monkey, but we're open to any further suggestions you may have.'

This completely stumped Livingstone who, lost for words, let the phone slip out of his hand onto the cradle, his mouth opening and closing like a beached fish.

'What the devil are we dealing with here?' he breathed, 'this is definitely one for the Boss,' and he reached for the phone again.

. . . .

Jack was walking home from school, thinking if he should call on Lucy and tell her about the fracas in the classroom, when he saw her walking towards him.

'Hi! I was just coming to see you; guess what happened at school today.'

'Poltergeist,' she said abruptly.

'Witch!' he retorted. 'Is there anything that goes on around here that you don't know about?'

'Not much, but we have to talk about this, it's a disturbing new development.'

'I'll say it is, it certainly disturbed Smithy's classroom, and as for Smithy, well I think he's destined for the teacher's home for the terminally disturbed.'

'Quick!' said Lucy ushering him to the rear of the house, 'Before anyone spots us.'

'Hey! You're good at this spy lark,' he teased.

Lucy ignored him and proceeded to the computer room while he followed on behind. 'Just remember my parents expect me home for tea at a certain time and you wouldn't want to attract attention to yourself by whisking me off to China or somewhere.'

'You really need to start thinking on a bigger scale,' she scolded and sat down at the computer.

'So what are we going to do?'

'Well, I felt the disturbances while I was in the other dimension, and I detected that the police are involved.'

'One policeman took statements, but I doubt very much if they're going to make any sense of it, he seemed totally nonplussed,' said Jack.

'He may be,' she said, 'but his superiors may have a different view of the matter; we have to put a stop to it before it gets out of hand.'

'How can we do that?' he said excitedly.

'We have to de-sensitise Megan and make her less of a target. This mischievous entity is obviously using her as a means of gaining access to our dimension. First we have to get this working,' she patted the laptop computer, 'this should give us some flexibility.'

'So she was right,' breathed Jack. 'I was going to talk to you about that.'

'What do you mean, who was right?'

'Megan. She said she thought she'd caused the classroom upheaval.'

'Mon dio!' exclaimed Lucy. 'This may be worse than I first thought.'

'Why?'

'Because she suspects she's the centre of this activity which makes her inquisitive and dangerous.'

'I don't understand,' he said, feeling helpless.

'Never mind now, let's get on with it.'

She switched on the main computer and set up the portal, then, taking the DVD and the laptop they proceeded down to the conservatory where the glowing blue sphere had begun to take shape. For some time she typed furiously on the laptop computer while the sphere danced and shimmered in the gathering dusk.

'There, that should do it,' she remarked finally. 'Now we should be able to control the portal using the laptop from anywhere we choose. Even if the police take away the computer upstairs, we will still be able to operate.'

As she said this, the sphere began to oscillate violently, she responded by typing further instructions into the laptop.

Crip appeared at her side looking worried, 'Rucy!' he shouted, 'Escape! Something velly bad happen!'

'What's the problem?' said Jack becoming alarmed.

The tension in her voice was obvious, 'I'm not sure, there seems to be something attempting to break through.'

'Switch it off,' said Jack nervously, 'we can always try again later.'

She handed him the laptop and moved towards the portal, peering into it. Crip began hopping about pulling at her shoe, 'Rucy! No! No!' he shouted.

'Just type in these numbers and . . . ,' her voice tailed off to a hushed whisper as the sphere gave a violent jerk and with a loud belch ejected a foul smelling object onto the conservatory floor.

To their horror the thing hoisted itself shakily onto four spidery legs and assumed a cat like arch. Jack nervously noted the spiked nail on each of the two long trailing toes of its feet. There was no doubting its intention as it turned to face them with obvious menace. The black slime dripped in gobbets from its spindly muscular body, while two rows of yellow teeth glinted in the glow of the portal as it tilted back its head and snarled viciously. They recoiled in revulsion as the cruel eyes surveyed them both down the pointed beak. Jack's body felt like lead, so that he was unable to move or think.

Lucy reacted first shouting, 'Switch off the portal! Press the escape button!'

He was jerked out of his stupor and, recovering from the shock, stabbed at the button, missing it in the poor light. Assuming it had not had the desired result; he dropped the laptop and rushed across the conservatory to confront the beast. Two more creatures tumbled out of the portal, one delivering a hefty blow to his midriff, sending him sprawling. The three vile creatures then turned on Lucy who gave out a piercing scream as they attacked her. She was no match for the combined efforts of the three monsters and ceased to struggle as they pinned her to the floor dripping excreta and raking with their claws at her exhausted body. Still panting from the blow, Jack struggled to his feet, intending to renew the conflict. He glanced at the sphere which was changing colour from blue to a glowing orange. It had begun to oscillate once more but this time more gently and a vague form had appeared in its depths. Jack tried to move across the room to Lucy but couldn't take his eyes off the shining orb where a face could now be seen. Hypnotised, he shuffled slowly towards the sphere.

'No!' screamed Lucy from her prone position, 'Press the escape button!' One of the demons slapped her around the head and she fell silent.

Two tawny coloured eyes with lion-like irises had now appeared in the portal. Jack moved closer, fascinated by the vision which was becoming clearer by the second. It was the image of a man with a flowing mane of ginger hair swept back from a broad forehead. The image pointed a finger at him and beckoned. Jack's mind began to swim and his body felt numb. He walked into the portal and disappeared!

. . . .

Convinced that her hallucinations were somehow connected with Jack and the strange Chinese girl, who had appeared from nowhere, Megan followed him once again as he left school. Dim memories of a conservatory were adding to her feelings that the answer was somehow to be found around the house where she had recovered from her faint. She shivered at the thought that it may indeed be, as she had jokingly remarked, haunted, but was determined to investigate whatever the consequences. She reasoned that she may have entered it after following Jack that evening.

She saw Lucy approaching before Jack did and swiftly hid behind a bush while they talked briefly. She watched them enter the garden and whispered to herself, 'so that's the house, now to check out the conservatory.'

She slipped around the back and dropping down on all fours peered through the conservatory window where the bottom of the blinds left a gap. *I was right, there is a conservatory,* she thought.

The room was in darkness and there was no activity that she could see. She decided to make her way into the house and trying the conservatory door found it to be unlocked. Shivering from cold and anxiety she gently opened the door and stealthily crept inside. She paused for a moment and listened intently. Footsteps and hushed voices could be heard approaching. As she turned to leave, the blue shining sphere began to materialise and the memory of the previous occasion came flooding back. Quickly she crept outside and knelt down once more to survey the scene through the gap in the blinds. Her excitement and curiosity aroused, she watched as the dreadful scene was played out as in a horror movie.

Shaking with fear she opened the door unseen and crouched behind a table as Lucy was set upon by the demons. She watched with terrible fascination as the lion face appeared in the orange orb and gave a gasp as Jack moved towards it, clearly incapable of controlling his actions.

'Press the escape button!' screamed Lucy, but it was too late, Jack had dropped the computer and was heading for the apparition. Megan grabbed it and pressed the escape button with a shaking finger. The sphere immediately disappeared with Jack in it. She gave a strangled cry and turned to see if Lucy could assist. The demons had vanished leaving a residue of evil smelling slime and the lifeless Lucy. Fighting back the urge to vomit, Megan dragged Lucy out of the conservatory and into the kitchen of the house where she lay slumped, still unconscious, on the floor.

CHAPTER 12

STILL SHAKING, SHE scrabbled around the kitchen wall until she found a light switch. Seeing a cup on the table she filled it with water and unceremoniously emptied it on Lucy's face. Lucy shuddered, opened her eyes and raised herself up onto one elbow, 'Where did you spring from?' she spluttered.

Megan's eyes flashed angrily, 'It's just as well for you that I did or you would be eaten alive by now,' she cried pointing to the bites on Lucy's arms and legs. 'What were those horrible things that were attacking you; are you practising black magic? What are you, the head witch in this coven?' she yelled, her jaw jutting accusingly.

'If you hadn't been so nosey in the first place none of this would have happened,' shouted Lucy, struggling to her feet and grimacing from the pain of her wounds. 'If you must know, I was trying to help you from causing any more chaos like you did in the classroom at school.'

Lucy slumped onto a chair, bowed forward with her head resting in her hands and stared disconsolately at the floor. 'No, I'm not a witch,' she said in a small tired voice.

'So it is true, that poltergeist was caused by me.'

'Yes.'

Megan realised Lucy was exhausted from her experience and, with an effort, swallowed her anger. 'I suppose we're not going to get anywhere by sniping at each other, and we have to make the best of it,' she relented, 'but why? How did it happen? What is going on?'

'You walked into my portal after you followed Jack and were attacked by some malevolent entity. It's a pity it never finished you off! Ugh!' she gasped, retching uncontrollably, 'If I don't get a shower soon I'll turn myself inside out.'

She ran upstairs throwing off her slime soaked clothes as she went. 'Where's Jack?' she shouted above the noise of the shower.

Megan followed her upstairs and sat on the toilet seat, 'I could ask you the same question. What have you done to him? He seems to have been gobbled up by your diabolical toy,' she sobbed.

Lucy's face appeared from behind the shower curtain wearing a shocked expression, 'You mean he went into the portal?' she gasped.

'If that's what you call that orange spherical thing, yes!'

'Orange?'

'Yes, with the face of a lion in it.'

'Lion?'

'Well, it may have been a parrot, which sounds more like your style,' she snapped waspishly.

'I thought you agreed to make the best of it,' countered Lucy.

'OK, I'm sorry, but what have you done to him?' wailed Megan.

'Let's find out,' said Lucy, stepping out of the shower. She wrapped a towel around herself and hurried into the computer room, trailing water from her long black hair and blood from the wounds on her legs.

In spite of her hostility Megan watched her with mounting admiration, *God: she's certainly a plucky devil*, she thought, *considering what she's just been through.*

'Hey! Hold on, you need some antiseptic on those wounds,' she cried waving a bottle she had found in the bathroom cabinet.

'OK fix me up while I investigate.'

While she worked at the computer, Megan dabbed antiseptic on her wounds and watched, fascinated, as she searched for some trace of Jack. She seemed completely impervious to the stinging pain of the antiseptic.

Megan jumped back, startled, as Crip appeared on the desk.

'What's that?' she exclaimed gaping incredulously at the paper clip.

Crip looked hurt and examined Megan suspiciously from lowered eyelids, 'Who this Rucy?'

'Jack's girlfriend, Megan,' said Lucy mischievously, and smiling to herself added, 'or she would very much like to be.'

'You're obviously feeling better,' said Megan, 'just find him and then we can get out of this house of horrors, talking paper clips, and demons and forget all about it.'

'I'm afraid you can't do that now,' said Lucy turning to face her.

'Why?'

'Because you've seen too much, and . . . ,' she paused, 'if you report anything, Jack may be put in danger.'

'That's a bit melodramatic isn't it?'

'It wasn't intended to be, but it happens to be the truth.'

Megan pointed an accusing finger: 'What has he got himself into to put himself in danger? Ugh! This is your fault; what have you been doing to him?'

Lucy ignored the outburst and turned back to the computer.

Megan slumped cross-legged on the bare floorboards and sat in frustrated silence while Lucy typed furiously and Crip paced back and forth on the desk. Finally she muttered, 'I don't know why I should believe anything you say, but I suppose I'd better go along with it . . . for now anyway.'

Lucy nodded appreciatively and Crip responded with, 'I herp you Mego.'

. . . .

Jack had thought his number was up. This was surely it. He was dying. Any ambition he may have harboured for his life plan was finished. His parents would be disappointed, particularly his father. He was a disembodied, floating consciousness in the vastness of space time where there was no pain, no feelings, nothing which could convince him of a bodily existence save for unsubstantiated memories. He was suddenly gripped by panic. Had he had a stomach it would surely have turned over as the realisation of his condition became apparent, he was alone, totally alone, and may be destined to be so for eternity. In some respects it was quite pleasant to be free from the nagging desires of the body, but this timeless, effortless, floating experience was offset by the diabolical feeling that he was the only entity alive. He had no eyes to see, but as he became accustomed to his condition he thought he could detect other entities filtering into his awareness from time to time, or was it wishful thinking? He tried to stabilise his mind by thinking back to the circumstances which had catapulted him into this situation. The scene in the conservatory was depicted in far more detail than would have been the case had he been using his eyes. Maybe, he thought because I don't have the encumbrance of a body everything was much clearer.

It was very curious but he suddenly began to feel more comfortable, the panic had subsided, it was now as though this was his more natural condition than that of physical existence and he was beginning to embrace it. He examined the scene in minute detail hoping to find clues which may help him return, there were none, but a human shape could be seen crouching outside the conservatory. In his mind's eye he tried to identify the mysterious form but could not and so he turned his attention to the apparition in the portal. He concentrated hard on the vision trying to identify its purpose. As he did so a word appeared in his mind, accompanied by a sound which was felt instead of heard, like the crashing of cymbals, 'Jerome', softly at first then louder, 'Jerome!'

Strangely, he could feel no fear in his present condition, and this perception gave him a confidence that he had never before experienced. He formed the question in his mind; 'Who are you, what do you want?'

There was no reply for what seemed like an eternity, and then in a hollow monotone, 'Beware, beware, God sees.'

Jack puzzled over this for a while then finally gave up, putting it to the back of his mind. The entity had long since disappeared and had been replaced with shimmering areas of continuously shifting coloured energy, the intensity of which would never have been possible to physical vision.

Perhaps, thought Jack, this is how our three dimensional world appears from another dimension.

He remembered something from his physics lessons about mass really being energy in a different form, and although you could transform one to the other, it was a universal law that you could never destroy energy.

The uneasy feeling of being watched came to him, a shadowy something lurking just out of reach. He remembered the last time he had that feeling was on his way to school on the morning all this began. What could it be: alter ego, guardian angel, God or Devil? Whatever it was, it was more real in his present condition. His mind wandered to the root of the whole business, Lucy's father, and he marvelled at the genius of the man and what he had accomplished.

Suddenly without warning there was a rushing sensation and the experience of sounds like chimes of massive bells. Everything became totally confused, his mind went blank and ceased to function.

As he regained consciousness he was aware of a bright light burning through his eyelids. He was lying on what felt like a rough mattress and around him he could hear the babble of excited conversation. He tried in vain to understand what was being said but the language was completely alien to him, so with a supreme effort he attempted to open his eyes and peer through the glare. A soft, musical, man's voice came close to his ear, 'Jack, you OK now, lie still, everything come back soon.'

What did he mean by that? He made to sit up, but nothing happened. He felt the skin of his forearm being pinched and something being pumped into his veins. His whole body felt as if it were being inflated like a balloon as the injection spread. Gradually his physical functions began to return and he opened his eyes. The kindly, weather-beaten, old face peering into his he instantly recognised as that of Lucy's father!

'Where am I,' he managed to mumble, through lips that felt as though he had just been to the dentist.

'Sh! Take easy, you in university,' said the Chinaman, 'we only had few minutes warning so could not prepare properly. It lucky Lucy had given us D.N.A. profile for you.'

Jack looked around as best he could from his prone position. Several white coated Chinese people were grouped around him all beaming excitedly.

Chu leaned forward, 'You are . . . ah . . . how you say? A celebrity!'

The group respectfully parted to accommodate a tall, dark suited man. His jet black hair glistened in the bright arc lamp as he bowed his head briefly towards Jack, then adjusting his black heavy framed spectacles he began to read from what looked like a prepared script. Jack understood none of it except for the very last statement, 'Wercome to China Jack. Prease enjoy stay.'

He didn't know how to respond so simply smiled at the man who beamed back at him. Chu and his colleagues joined in, eagerly clapping and smiling. Chu leaned forward, took his hand and shook it vigorously, 'You are first person to be teleported from one place to another. Congratulations!'

Apart from a curious tingling sensation in his legs he felt physically normal, but his mind was unable to grasp the situation. He remembered thinking about Lucy and the demons, the figure crouching in the shadows, then of Chu and suddenly he was here!

'How did I get here?' he managed to mumble.

'You probably thought . . . ah . . . about me,' answered Chu.

'And that brought me here?'

'You only have to think to make it so when in other dimension, of course not . . . ah . . . always possible.'

'So I am really in China?' said Jack hesitantly.

'Of course you . . . ah . . . are in China, in university laboratory.'

The excited group of scientists had been herded away by the dark suited man leaving Jack and Chu alone. Jack reached out and gripped Chu's chubby arm, 'I have to get back home.'

'But must stay for little while, we . . . ah . . . celebrate our achievement.'

'Chu!' said Jack emphatically, 'You don't understand, if I'm not back soon my parents may call the police, which could lead them to Lucy again.'

He suddenly remembered Lucy pinned to the floor by the demons and his heart leaped in his chest as he reared up from the bed. 'How is she? She was being attacked by those vile things.'

Chu rested his hand lightly on Jack's shoulder, 'Calm down Jack, Lucy OK. She tell me . . . ah . . . about attack and your concern about things like this happening. We investigate, but you right, you must get back. First you must have instruction to keep safe in other dimension. Then organise transit properly. For now rest . . . ah . . . a little, here drink, you may be dehydrated.' Chu handed him a warm cup of tea which Jack gratefully sipped.

. . . . ah . . . .

It did not take long for Lucy to become exhausted. The experience with the demons had taken its toll and she was approaching the edge of despair when suddenly an email came through from her father. It read, "Congratulations on your first transfer of consciousness, Jack's here, are you OK?" Lucy was both relieved and elated and sent an immediate response then translated the message for Megan.

'Where is here?' inquired Megan.

'I suppose I shall have to tell you sometime,' she said reluctantly, 'he's in China.'

'Is this another one of your silly games?' cried Megan, 'Tell me the truth.'

With a great effort Lucy put her antagonism aside and repeated evenly, 'I'm telling you the truth, he was teleported and *is* in China.'

Megan stood up and went to the window. 'Stupid game so it is,' she muttered and made to open the curtains in order to look out onto the street, expecting to see Jack strolling along towards the house.

'No! Don't open the curtains!' Lucy shouted.

Megan started back from the window, 'Why not? What are you afraid of . . . ghosts? I suppose in your crazy world, where you conjure up demons; ghosts and teleportation are normal.'

'That's right.'

'And you still say he was teleported to China?' asked Megan, her eyes growing wide with wonder.

'Well, not intentionally. Fortunately my father's portal was available in China and Jack must have allowed that possibility to enter his mind, maybe without even realising it.'

'I don't understand,' said Megan resignedly.

'In other dimensions,' explained Lucy, 'when you think of something, it becomes so. Jack probably diverted himself to my father's portal without knowing he'd done it.'

Megan was silent for some time as Lucy's words began to sink in.

'So how do we get him back?'

'Probably not for some time, my father and his associates will want to celebrate their achievement. It is the first time a human has been transferred, they must be very excited and will want to make a big fuss of him.'

'But he's got school tomorrow and what about his parents?'

'Pah!' said Lucy impatiently, 'People are always concerned with unimportant things. This is a great achievement by Father and it should be celebrated properly.'

'Ok, so it isn't a problem for you if Jack's parents report him missing to the police?'

'Can't you tell them he's sleeping over at a friend's tonight?'

'They wouldn't believe me and in any case why should I lie to them?' she said, her arms folded and a stubborn expression on her face. 'I can't believe I'm having this conversation. You've transported him off to China and you don't want his parents to know?'

'Ugh! You're impossible,' shouted Lucy, 'why did you ever have to interfere?'

'Because I worry about Jack which is something you obviously do not do, otherwise you wouldn't have mislaid him so easily,' she said icily.

Lucy was too tired to argue any more. She swung round to the computer and began typing rapidly.

'What are you doing?'

'I'm looking for a way to de-sensitise you.'

'What do you mean?'

'Well, I think you're being used as a means of gaining access to this dimension by those disgusting creatures.' She shuddered as she spoke and for a moment Megan couldn't help feeling some sympathy with her, remembering her own horrific experience in her bedroom when the wallpaper came to life.

'You mean like a medium, like at a séance?'

'Something like that,' replied Lucy.

'So how do you de-sensitise me?'

'I don't quite know yet, that's something I have to work out.'

'Oh charming, so it's a guinea pig I'm going to be is it?'

'Pig? Now there's a thought,' muttered Lucy mischievously, 'well my dear, if I turn you into a pig, I need have nothing more to do with you,' she continued, with a faint smile.

Megan overheard the remark; 'Where have I heard that before. Oh yes! I remember; when Alice falls down a rabbit hole into a crazy world, where nothing is as it seems? That's very appropriate so it is!'

'You should know all about "Wonderland", thinking that Jack could ever fall for you,' snapped Lucy.

Megan turned away, tears welling in her eyes. Suddenly she spun around, 'I hate you for doing this to him,' she spat out, 'why did you have to interfere in our lives?'

'You're an ungrateful nuisance,' said Lucy, 'I'm trying to help you get out of the mess *you* created by wandering into *my* portal. Those things will keep returning in some way or another because *you* are attracting them! And it's me who almost got clawed to death!'

'And who saved you?' shouted Megan.

'Do you want to spend the rest of your life with three loathsome creatures for company trying to pass them off as family pets? It could have a disastrous effect on your social life . . . and your relationship with Jack.'

Megan smiled involuntarily at the thought of the demons being kept on leads as pets. Lucy, seeing this, allowed herself a chuckle and they began to giggle at her description of Megan's possible fate.

Lucy knew that the disturbances of the last hour or so would not go unnoticed by the neighbours. She motioned at the adjacent house.

'Shush!' she managed through suppressed laughter, 'we mustn't attract attention to ourselves.'

'Too late for that, they probably think we're having a late Halloween party,' said Megan.

'With real demons!' laughed Lucy.

As Lucy assembled Megan's quantum fingerprint she explained the mechanics of it all to her inquisitive new colleague. When she had finished she exclaimed triumphantly, 'I didn't know that was possible. Now I have another tool which I can use to defend us against mischievous entities. You should be OK, no more visits from *them*.' She slumped back in the chair and closed her eyes.

Megan paced around the room, becoming increasingly agitated. She glanced at Lucy who appeared to be fast asleep. After her exhausting experience she didn't have the heart to wake her. *What am I to tell Jack's parents, if we can't get him back tonight?* She thought

She determined to explore the rest of the house with the intention of finding Lucy's bed and transferring her there. She had completed a tour of the upstairs with no success when she heard Lucy calling. Quickly returning to the computer room she found her totally refreshed and working at the computer again.

'I thought you were out for the night, I was going to put you to bed, but I couldn't find one,' she said.

'I don't have one.'

'So where do you sleep?'

'I don't need very much. I occasionally have a nap in the chair.'

Megan stared at her in disbelief, 'Don't you ever have a proper sleep?' she gasped.

'I meditate instead,' she said, 'it's just as good, and takes less time, besides I have to keep a watch out for the police.'

'Why? Are you afraid of them?'

'No,' said Lucy defiantly, 'it's just that they want to send me back to China, and if they succeed I won't be able to continue my work here.'

'Your work? What exactly is that? Who do you work for? Beelzebub?' she sniffed.

'Well you won't believe anything I tell you so I'll let Jack explain when I get him back.'

'So you are going to get him back?'

'Yes, I'll just have to be a party pooper,' she said turning back to the keyboard.

CHAPTER 13

NIGEL DAWKINS LOOKED up from his newspaper, 'You're late,' he said accusingly, 'you're mother and I have been worrying about you, where have you been?'

'I'm sorry,' said Jack, 'I went round to a friend for a cup of tea after school.' He hoped that the conversation would end there but Nigel persisted.

'Where did you go?'

'I went where you would normally go for a decent cup of tea, China of course!'

Nigel sniffed, 'Smart arse,' he said, 'and I suppose you came back at the speed of light?'

'Pretty much I expect,' said Jack with a faint smile, 'how did you know?'

Nigel shook his newspaper in agitated fashion, grumbled something about lippy teenagers and retreated behind it.

His mother was not so easily dismissed, 'What's that strange smell?' she said, as they sat down to slightly overcooked dinner.

'Smell?' remarked Jack looking bemused and investigating the contents of his plate, 'I can't smell anything.'

'Well it's coming from you,' she said accusingly as she leaned over and sniffed his hair. 'Carbolic!' she exclaimed triumphantly.

Jack's mind was racing, *how to explain this?* 'Swimming! That's what you can smell ... yes, I've been swimming. You can probably smell the chlorine.'

'Doesn't smell like chlorine to me,' she muttered dubiously, and sat down frowning.

Jack hated keeping secrets from his parents. In spite of the continuous rumbling row about his future, he held them in high regard and had no desire to see them hurt. To avoid any further discomfort he went to his room after tea. He sat on his bed and stared blankly at the wall and revisited the evening's events.

He had walked into the portal as if in a trance and that troubled him greatly. Just when Lucy needed him most, he had let her down. There was no recrimination, however, on Lucy's part when she brought him back, nevertheless the doubt remained, and he determined to be a safe pair of hands in the future.

To his great surprise, he had stepped out of the portal to be greeted by Megan who threw her arms around him in relief while Lucy looked on in mild amusement. Her business-like manner made Megan feel uncomfortable and she had quickly contained her emotional reaction. Secretly, he had felt flattered, but it was Lucy's aloof behaviour that had left him with the ache he could neither describe nor dismiss.

His alarm on finding Megan at the house was compounded when he saw Lucy's wounds. She explained how Megan had saved her from the demons and that they had decided to call a truce in their behaviour to each other in the future. Given that Megan was now aware of the situation, he had considered it to be a sensible arrangement.

It had all happened so quickly he was afraid that it really hadn't happened at all and he would have liked to have spent more time with Chu. Circumstances, however, required no unusual behaviour at home, so now he sat in his bedroom after the most bizarre event of his life unable to speak to anyone about it. Feeling disconsolate he switched on his computer and was immediately confronted by Lucy in a high state of excitement.

'Jack! The police are outside my house and I'm afraid they are going to come in at any moment.'

'How long have they been there?'

'About fifteen minutes.'

'Can you escape through the portal?'

'I daren't risk it, if they are outside the conservatory as I'm going into it, they'll see everything.'

'Do you think you can slip out without being noticed?'

'I'll try, why? What are you planning?'

'I don't know yet, I'll think of something once you've got away, but you can't afford to let them arrest you. I'll meet you outside Megan's house in twenty minutes,' he said with more confidence than he would have dared before recent events. 'Oh, and bring the laptop,' he added.

He ran downstairs to the hall, made a quick telephone call to Megan, an excuse to his parents and left for their rendezvous.

Lucy already had a small holdall packed with her few belongings. She kept it hidden in the attic where it was unlikely to be discovered. She crammed in the laptop and started to make her way downstairs but stumbled over the clothes she had cast off earlier. 'Drat!' she said to herself,

'I'll have to take these with me. The police will certainly find them if I don't.' She found a plastic carrier bag in the kitchen stuffed the clothes into it, tiptoed into the lounge and peered out of the window at the police car parked a little way down the street. She could clearly see the two men in the orange glare of the street lamp. They appeared to be arguing about something suggested by their jerky arm movements. She didn't hang about to see any more. She padded silently through the conservatory trying to ignore the foetid smell left by the monsters, locked the door from the outside and made for the water butt at the bottom of the garden. She placed the key in its hiding place, turned around and almost fell over DC Collins. Instinctively, she made to run off but her foot slipped on the wet grass and she fell on one knee. Collins grabbed her with a firm grip and hauled her to her feet.

'Well, well, well, so you do exist after all,' he said triumphantly. 'I think we need to have a little chat,' he continued, as he steered her towards the front of the house.

Lucy was as surprised as Collins at what happened next. Two demons appeared from nowhere, leaped onto his back and pitched him headfirst into the shrubbery alongside the path, where he remained struggling and yelling. Lucy, seeing her opportunity seized her bags and ran off down the street and was gone before the policeman could give chase. The unfortunate Collins finally managed to escape from the beasts, but not before they had taken several chunks of his flesh with their needle sharp teeth and powerful little jaws. They disappeared as quickly as they had come leaving the distraught policeman to stagger back to the car and the waiting DI Livingstone.

He yanked open the door and threw himself on the back seat. Livingstone turned around to survey the muddy, bloody, dishevelled policeman.

'She made short work of you then?' he said sarcastically. 'It just serves you right for disobeying orders which were, in case it's slipped your memory, "observe do not investigate".'

'But someone may have been murdered,' protested Collins, 'the neighbours reported seeing strange lights and hearing desperate screaming.'

'It seems to me the only person who was close to being murdered tonight was you,' said Livingstone acidly. 'Fancy allowing yourself to be set upon by that mere slip of a girl, seven stone, if that, and you a great hulking, full grown man.'

Livingstone peered closely at the bites inflicted by the beasts, 'God! You stink.' He retched and threw open the car door to get some fresh air. 'How did you get those bites, and that smell, have you been rolling in manure?'

'I didn't get a good look at them. They jumped me from behind. It may have been two dogs,' he suggested, looking ruefully at the state of his clothes.

'Dogs don't smell like that,' returned Livingstone. Let's have a look around the house now the bird's fled the coop and we no longer have anything to survey. How am I going to explain this to the Boss?'

'Don't know,' mumbled Collins apologetically, 's'pose you'll have to blame me.'

'How very astute,' agreed Livingstone.

After a half hour of fruitless searching, they were once more standing in the computer room. 'That's amazing,' said Livingstone.

'What?' said Collins, from the depths of depression.

'Everything is exactly as we left it and yet she's obviously been living here. Where does she eat, sleep, and wash her clothes?'

'Could account for that horrendous smell in the conservatory?' asked Collins timidly.

'I don't think so, but I do think we have a remarkably determined and talented young lady on our hands. Mm! Smell and dogs, an ideal combination,' he muttered, 'don't you think? That's it!' he said triumphantly.

Collins was confused, he was vainly hoping that he may be able to go home, dress his wounds and have a bath. It was not to be. Livingstone was now literally on the scent.

'Get on that mobile of yours and get a dog handler here with a bloodhound, pronto,' he said. Collins groaned; it was obviously going to be a long night.

The dog and handler duly appeared some time later, but the dog refused to enter the conservatory.

'Unusual for a dog,' remarked the handler as it sat on its haunches looking at its master with pleading eyes and making a peculiar coughing noise down its nose.

Finally it was persuaded to follow the scent which Lucy had left behind. At a junction in the road the dog appeared to be confused, rushing this way and that. The scent being detected again the dog set off at a fair trot trailing three policemen to the school fields. Being outside the range of the street lights, Collins switched on his torch and followed first behind the handler and dog, which was now becoming very excited. Suddenly the dog made a detour into some bushes and stopped beside the body of a young woman lying face down on the ground, her long waist length black hair spread like a fan over her naked back.

Collins waited for his heavily panting boss to catch up, 'It looks like the end of the road boss; she's got a spear like thing sticking out of the back of her neck. There's not much chance of her being alive with all this blood loss.'

'Poor devil!' remarked Livingstone, and for the first time Collins heard an emotional quiver in his voice.

'Get an ambulance down here,' he said, recovering quickly. 'See if there's any sign of her clothes.'

Collins turned away to make the phone call and was promptly sick in the bushes.

CHAPTER 14

MEGAN AND JACK had been impatiently waiting for some time outside Megan's house.

'She should be here by now,' said Jack in worried tones, 'it's not that far.'

'Maybe the police have arrested her,' said Megan, 'what were you planning?'

'I'm not sure yet,' he said as he sat down on the low wall bordering the front of the house, 'I don't think it's safe for her to stay in that house on her own, particularly with the police constantly sniffing around.'

She joined him on the wall and they sat in silence for a few minutes considering the problem.

'Listen now, I have an idea,' said Megan enthusiastically. 'What if I ask her to stay at our house for a while until the fuss dies down?'

'Can you do that? What about your parents? What would you tell them?'

'Mam and Dad will be alright see, once I've told them the sob story of how she's a university student kicked out of her flat by an unscrupulous landlord.'

Jack grinned, 'You certainly know how to spin a yarn,' he said, 'but what about Mandy, your sister, little girls can be very inquisitive?'

'Oh! Don't worry about her luvvy, I know how to control her.'

Jack stood up once more, 'Where is she?' he murmured, half to himself.

'Now there's a thing, fancy you worrying about a girl,' said Megan, with more than a hint of jealousy.

Jack ignored the comment and began pacing back and forth. 'Sooner or later, either your parents, or more likely Mandy, will see more than they should, it's very risky.'

'Well, boyo, I would hope that while she was with us, she wouldn't go in for anything obvious, like witches covens or ritual slaughter.'

Suddenly a soft voice behind them interrupted their conversation, 'Sorry I'm late, I'm afraid I had a bit of a confrontation with the police and then had to make a detour to put them off the scent, or they would have followed me here.' Lucy stepped out of the shadows and joined them under the orange glow of the street lamp.

'What was the problem?' asked Jack.

She described what had happened, and then paused thoughtfully, 'It was almost as though those monsters were helping me to escape. They didn't touch me, but I think they made a nasty mess of the policeman.'

'They probably didn't like the taste of you the first time,' Megan offered.

Lucy pursed her lips, 'You mean I was too sweet for them,' she pouted.

'Ugh!' retorted Megan, with feeling.

'Seriously though,' she said, 'it was weird, like the cavalry arriving just in time. I suppose I'll have to wait until the police give up before I can go home.'

'Hang on, Megan's had an idea, see what you think,' said Jack. With that Megan explained her plan.

'You have a two year old sister?' said Lucy screwing up her nose, 'Another one like you?'

'Hey!' interjected Jack, 'I thought you two had agreed to be friends.'

'Whoa!' cried Megan, 'That's a bit strong. We have simply put hostilities aside . . . for now.'

Lucy nodded her agreement, 'Well I must admit having a few regular meals appeals to me, but I've never had much to do with children before.'

'Oh come on,' said Megan, 'I'm sure they have children in China. And after all, you're only just an adult yourself.'

'Too many,' agreed Lucy, 'OK, we'll give it a try, but only for a little while until I'm sure the police have cleared off.'

Megan's mother, Rosie, intercepted them as they entered the house via the kitchen.

'Now there's cosy, you two been out together?' she began, then stopped abruptly as she caught sight of Lucy.

Lucy noted her strange appearance. Without her support stockings, her knotted blue veins were clearly visible. She wore a garish, green, knitted, knee length cardigan over her sagging night-dress which was constantly threatening to slide off her big boned angular frame as she moved. Two large pink rollers were ineffectual in containing the bush of rampant dyed blond hair through which the black roots were visible. A red woollen hat perched precariously on top of them was the cherry on a gaudy cake.

'Who's this then?' she said politely enough.

Megan launched into her explanation with gusto, while Rosie busied herself checking her visitor's appearance.

'Oh luvvy!' she burst out suddenly, 'Look at you, bitten all over, so you are.'

Megan, quick to note the possibilities, cut in, 'Yes Ma the landlord's dog did that.'

'Oh! My darling,' gushed Rosie, 'of course you must stay,' and she ushered Lucy into the front room, where Megan's father was busy, feet on a groaning coffee table watching television and drinking beer. He rose unsteadily and attempted to focus on the visitor. Swaying slightly, he shambled across to greet her, nudging the heavy dining table out of his way and giving Jack a cursory grunt as he went.

'What's your name darling?' said Rosie as the lumbering giant approached.

'Brenda!' cut in Megan.

Jack sniggered softly, but Lucy remained impassive.

'Brenda's going to stay with us for a while Bobby boy, so you behave yourself now, see?'

Bobby's brooding brow, brightened momentarily. 'You stay as long as you like luv' he said, throwing a heavy arm around her shoulders and squeezing her to him. Lucy gasped as the air was crushed from her slight body. Rosie leaned over and swiped Bobby across the face.

'I said behave yourself Bobby bach.'

He lurched back from the force of the blow, 'I was only being friendly missus,' he spluttered through thick lips.

'Don't mind him darling, there's no harm in him, let's get you installed in the box room,' said Rosie.

Megan smiled at Lucy, who grimaced in return as they both followed Rosie upstairs. Jack was left with Bobby's bruised ego which very quickly retreated into its alcoholic haze. He politely refused the offered beer as Bobby slumped into his chair and promptly fell asleep. Thunderous snoring drifted upstairs as Jack made his way to the box room where he found Lucy had already installed her meagre belongings and Rosie had disappeared. Megan sat on the small bed, Lucy cross-legged on the floor.

'Brenda?' exploded Jack.

'It was all I could think of at the time,' said Megan with a mischievous grin, 'anyway what's wrong with that? It's a fine name.'

'Maybe it's OK in the Welsh valleys but not for a Chinese girl.'

Lucy was not amused, 'It's no matter, I'll go as soon as the police lose interest in my house, I'll check it out tomorrow,' she said, patting the laptop.

She was exhausted, so after a spell of extended yawning Megan and Jack left her in peace to indulge in the luxury of a real bed.

Jack sat in a chair by the side of the bed in Megan's room and flicked casually through the pages of her art book as they discussed how their lives had changed.

'I have to admit, I didn't quite believe what I was being told, it just seemed like so much hot air of the sort spouted by Smithy. But then it actually happened and I found myself in China.'

'What was it like? It must have been fantastic to be out of your body and free to go anywhere.'

He screwed up his nose, 'Well the first problem is you don't have anywhere to go, no reference points you see. You don't even know where you're starting from. That's something we're so used to in three dimensions, that we don't even notice it, until it's not there.'

'That's impossible to imagine,' agreed Megan propping her pillow against the bed head and looking wide eyed, like a child waiting for a bed-time story.

'At first it was an awful, lonely experience, thinking I would never see anybody again. How long it lasted I have no idea, you have no feel for time in other dimensions. Strangely though, that passed and I felt quite at home, it was as though being there was more natural than being here. Almost as if this existence, in the third dimension, is a dream and there, whatever *there* means, is reality.'

'Did you see any other life?' queried Megan.

'Well, of course I couldn't see because I didn't have any eyes, but I had a heightened sense of feeling which means I could produce images in my mind which represent things that exist there.'

'You mean a sort of hallucination?'

'Yes something like that I guess. I conjured up something very curious when I tried to remember what happened in the conservatory . . . ,' his voice trailed off as he stared disbelievingly at a page of the book through which he had been browsing and his hands began to shake with excitement. 'That's it!' he finally managed to blurt out.

'What?'

'It's a proverb,' he said, trying to stay calm.

'What are you talking about?' she shouted in frustration, 'Stop talking in riddles and tell me.'

'Look! Look at this painting here,' he stabbed a finger at the page.

Megan craned around to look over his shoulder, 'Yes what about it?'

'You see that proverb written on the "Table Top of the Seven Deadly Sins"?'

'Cave . . . Cave . . . Deus vivit,' read Megan out loud.

'"Beware . . . Beware . . . God sees", see here, the translation of the Latin underneath,' he said excitedly.

'So what?'

'That's what Jerome said to me when I was in the other dimension.'

'Who's Jerome?'

'I think he's the lion face that appeared in the portal shortly before I was sucked into it.'

'So what is that to do with Hieronymous Bosch?' said Megan, pointing to the title page and handing the book back to him.

For a while he didn't answer, as he busily leafed through the pages of the book. Finally he gave a triumphant cry, 'That's it! He was christened Jerome Van Aken and later changed his name to Hieronymous Bosch.'

'So you're saying that we have been having visitations from a man who painted these pictures five hundred years ago.'

'Looks very much like it' he said.

Megan shuddered as she sat on the bed with her arms wrapped around a pillow and her knees pulled up to her chin, 'Jack, I'm scared.'

'No need to be,' he said, trying to make light of it, 'I've met him, spoken with him, he's a pussy cat, really he is.'

'Don't bach,' she murmured, 'this is serious. Have you looked at those pictures he painted, I mean really looked?'

He picked up the book and examined some of the paintings more closely. 'Decapitated bodies being chopped into pieces and fed into mincing machines, frying pans full of people being cooked; people stabbed with various knives and spears; All manner of horrendous torture. Everywhere monsters similar to those we saw in the conservatory' he said.

'Exactly! If you ask me they're the product of a deranged mind. I don't want to have that book in my room anymore.'

'You're right. I'll take it home and study it more closely. Lucy said something about desensitizing you; did she manage to do that?'

'Yes, she did but she threatened to turn me into a pig! Imagine! After I saved her from being eaten alive, that was all the thanks I got. However did you get mixed up with a witch like her?'

'I'll tell you later but for now, you should be alright. So if Jerome's not using you, who or what is he using now, and why?' he said thoughtfully.

'What do you mean?' she said becoming alarmed again.

'Those goblin things, appeared again tonight and according to Lucy, rescued her from the police, why on earth would they do that?'

She sneaked another look at the book and pointed to one of the paintings, 'Oh God!' she said, 'They look just like that!'

The malevolent beast in the painting was instantly recognisable to them. They speculated for some time as to how and why this five hundred-year-old entity should manifest itself and use these creatures, without reaching any conclusions. Finally they decided that more research was required and this would be best carried out in the school library.

Jack left for home with the book tucked under his arm and Megan settled down to a nightmare strewn sleep.

They agreed to meet in the library during a free period the next day at school. Jack had taken the book to school with him and it was immediately spotted by Chalky White at registration.

'You interested in art,' he said, 'or just torture?'

'Maybe both,' replied Jack curtly, and not wishing to prolong the conversation, left for the library.

When Megan arrived he had already assembled the library's meagre collection of books about Hieronymous Bosch. 'OK, I'll tell you what I've learned so far,' he whispered. 'Most of these,' he indicated the pile, 'agree that he was a very religious person who lived in the fifteenth century, and was famous for his paintings depicting the sins of man and the inevitable punishment of eternal damnation resulting from them. He was very much into this punishment business. It strikes me he was not so much religious as a fetishist, anyway that's just my opinion, but look at these pictures of demons and hideous monsters torturing their victims.'

Megan opened a book at random. She quickly realised the book she owned was only a brief glimpse of the total work by Bosch. She shuddered at the sight of the horrors depicted and quickly closed the book.

'I don't need to see any more. What else is he capable of if he can produce things like that?' she said quietly.

'That's a worry I know,' he said, 'particularly when you see his obsession with torture. But if we're going to deal with him, and it looks as though we have no choice, we have to know what his motives were, or rather, are.'

'What do *you* think he's after?'

'I think that while he was alive, in spite of the good press he had about his efforts to save humanity from itself, he was very much into the pleasures of the physical things rather than the spiritual. He'll probably want to continue those tendencies if he's found a way to access the physical world again.'

'I think you're probably right,' she said forlornly, 'he was screwed up when he was alive, so what he's like now, after five hundred years of pent up frustration, doesn't bear thinking about.'

Jack frowned, 'Time doesn't register there. I think all those nasty thoughts he harboured during his life,' he flicked a finger at the book, 'will be very fresh in his mind, as if it were yesterday. He knew deep down that he was capable of the worst excesses whether he committed them or not, and he was really anticipating his own punishment with these paintings.'

'Sort of a self fulfilling prophecy?' she said.

'Yes, I could be wrong but it looks like we're dealing with a thoroughly nasty character here. It's a pity he's dead, you can't very well do much to him when he's in that condition, can you?'

They fell silent for a while as they digested these new possibilities. Meanwhile Chalky had slipped into the library unnoticed and had sat down behind them.

Megan broke the silence, 'I don't see that we can do very much, he's got all the forces of evil available to him, but they exist in a different dimension.'

'Lucy may be able to help,' Jack said finally. 'We'll ask her after school tonight.'

Jack rose from the table as the bell rang signalling the beginning of the next lesson and was startled to see Chalky sitting behind him, apparently immersed in a book.

They left the library wondering if he had been deliberately eavesdropping but concluded that as they had been talking in low whispers, so as not to disturb the other occupants, he would not have heard very much.

That afternoon a disturbing rumour began to circulate Greystone Grammar. In the true tradition of rumour creation, its source could not be determined, but its validity was confirmed when, at three o'clock, the whole school was assembled in the hall.

The Headmaster raised his arms as he approached the front of the stage, calming the excited chatter of a thousand pupils to an expectant hush. His sombre mood was detected by all. He turned and indicated the thick set dishevelled figure standing nervously at the side of the stage, 'This is Detective.Inspector. Livingstone, who is going to speak to you about a very serious matter,' he said, and sat down.

This was an incredibly brief statement for him as he would not normally use one word where several would do. This departure from normal behaviour served to heighten the already charged atmosphere, and a ripple of excited conversation ran through the hall. Livingstone shuffled to the edge of the stage. The afternoon winter sun streamed through the windows directly onto his portly figure and into his eyes. He hesitated, blinking in the light.

'Somebody close a curtain,' yelled a teacher.

'His light's out already,' chimed a young voice, to the accompaniment of suffused titters.

The instruction duly carried out, Livingstone cleared his throat and began in ponderous police fashion; 'There has been a serious incident on the school playing field. An Asian girl approximately nineteen years old with black waist length hair has been murdered. The victim is, I believe, not known to you.' An excited buzz of conversation drowned out any further statement from the policeman.

'Quiet please' said the Headmaster and the sound of muted conversations gradually died away.

Livingstone continued, 'There are two things I want you to do for me. If anyone can remember seeing anything unusual or suspicious in that area last night at approximately nine thirty, please see me before you leave and secondly, do not walk home alone.' With that he turned and shuffled back to the rear of the stage.

Jack and Megan exchanged worried glances. As the level of conversation began to rise again, Megan whispered; 'Lucy shook off the police around that time, didn't she?'

Jack nodded and swiftly guided Megan out of the hall, 'That's a hell of a coincidence, how many Asian girls do you suppose were in that area at that time of night?'

As they sat down on a wall outside the school to gather their thoughts before going home, Dipper ambled up and greeted them, 'Hey you two, together again? You'll have the whole school talking.'

'Don't be an arse Brian,' said Jack, hoping he might continue on his way.

'I've just been talking to Chalky,' Dipper continued, 'he's a strange one isn't he? I could swear that yesterday the index finger of his left hand was missing, today it seems as though the other hand is missing a finger; anyway, he says this Chinese girl may have lived locally.'

Jack stared at him in surprise.

'What?' exclaimed Dipper, 'What did I say?'

'Nothing, nothing at all,' cut in Jack quickly, 'what else did he say?'

Dipper's face became conspiratorial as he leaned towards them, 'He says she was probably a drug dealer who got on the wrong side of her boss.'

Jack and Megan exchanged relieved glances, 'That seems a likely explanation,' agreed Jack.

'Anyway, I can't stay here playing gooseberry, got to get home before the killer strikes again,' said Dipper cheerfully. 'See ya!'

After Dipper had left, Jack turned to Megan, 'How did he know?'

'How did who know what?'

'How did Chalky know she was Chinese?'

'That policeman said so, didn't he?'

'No! He said she was Asian.'

They fell silent for a moment.

'What do you think is going on?' asked Megan.

'I don't know,' he confessed, 'but that's too much of a coincidence to be ignored. Just a minute though, I remember Lucy telling me that she produced a duplicate of herself when she fooled the police into thinking they had deported her. Perhaps she did that again.'

'Would she have had time while she was running away from the police? It seems a bit over the top just to make sure they followed the wrong trail, and anyway if that were so, who killed the duplicate Lucy?'

Jack considered what she had just said, it made sense. It was unlikely that Lucy should go to that much trouble, and anyway she could have done the same thing days ago, she always knew the police were trying to find her. Then who did produce the duplicate to kill it, and why?

'When the demons attacked Lucy, they drew her blood and D.N.A.,' he said. 'What if Jerome has discovered how to duplicate humans from that information?'

'Do you think that's possible?'

'We can't count it out,' he nodded.

'OK, so why would he produce it, and then kill it?'

An awful thought hit Jack, which he was almost afraid to suggest, yet he knew he must, 'What about this?' he started, choosing his words carefully. 'Jerome rescues Lucy from the police using his infernal devils. As she flees he produces a duplicate, kills the *real* Lucy so that she poses no threat to himself. Then he has a completely obedient copy that he can use to carry out his dodgy activities, whatever they may be. In addition the police will no longer be interested in Lucy's work as she no longer exists and will not be led to him through her.'

Megan sat on the wall as if she had been turned to stone. Suddenly she jumped to her feet with a strangled cry, 'Mandy!' With Jack at her side she ran home, fearing the worst, every step of the way.

CHAPTER 15

'IT JUST DOESN'T add up Boss,' said Collins, when I stumbled into her outside the house she was fully clothed. When we found her a short time later in the field, she hadn't a stitch on her, not even shoes, and yet we can't find any clothing at all. She was killed with a spear of all things, and the way she was laid out with no apparent sign of a struggle, not even a blade of grass disturbed, would make you think she welcomed it.'

'Your right of course,' Livingstone agreed wearily, 'it beats me; anything from Pathology?'

'They've only done a preliminary examination so far. Death was caused by neck wound to the jugular, very clinical they said, almost professional.'

Livingstone scratched his head and circumnavigated the office once more, 'It gets worse, why would anyone put out a contract on a harmless child like her, and with a spear of all things?'

'Ah! They do have something to say about that,' ventured Collins, 'they said it was the type often used in Europe in The Middle Ages.'

'Oh! That's very useful, thank you Collins.'

He slumped into his chair rested his chins on clenched fists and gazed at the phone.

The phone rang; both men started as if stung. Collins grabbed the receiver, 'It's for you, Johnson from the Path lab,' he said handing it to Livingstone.

The voice on the telephone said, 'D.I. Livingstone I presume?'

Johnson sounds too cheerful, thought Livingstone, *that usually means he's come up with something he knows will screw me up.* 'Cut the jokes Pathy, what's the news?' he grunted.

'You're going to love this one,' chortled Johnson, 'we've just emptied the contents of her stomach, and guess what?'

'Get on with it Pathy, I'm feeling sick already' he snapped.

'We've found a whole rat in there.'

'A what,' exclaimed the astonished policeman?

'A rat; you know one of those small furry rodents with a leg at each corner, long tail, beady eyes . . . .'

'All right, don't go on.'

Livingstone spun around in his chair and fixed Collins with an anxious glare, 'What date is it Collins?'

He glanced at the calendar, 'November the fifteenth' he said looking puzzled.

'So it's *not* April the first?'

Johnson butted in at the other end of the telephone, 'I'm telling you the truth, a whole rat with hardly a tooth mark on it.'

'So how did it get in there?' said Livingstone, knowing even as he said it that he should not have asked.

'Thankfully,' breathed Johnson, 'that's for you to find out. I've done my bit, now it's over to you.'

'Anything else?' Livingstone could feel numbness creeping into his mind and he wanted to get rid of Johnson as quickly as possible.

'Nothing much else, except that her fingernails were extremely brittle, probably something to do with her poor diet,' added Johnson as a parting shot.

'Thanks Johnson!' He slammed down the phone, unable to take any more mocking banter. He turned to Collins hoping for inspiration, but quickly decided that would be a hopeless exercise. No, he would have to discuss this directly with his boss. *How in heavens name*, he thought to himself, *does a nineteen-year old girl swallow a whole rat in one gulp, and then end up assassinated with a medieval spear?* 'It beggars belief,' he muttered as he knocked on Smiley's office door.

. . . .

Megan and Jack were panting heavily as they reached the front door. They flung it open and ran upstairs to the box room, fearing what they may find inside. Megan's heart was in her mouth as she nudged the door open nervously.

They were confronted with a picture of innocent play. Lucy and Mandy were lying on the floor on their stomachs happily discussing where they should try to fit the piece of jigsaw, which Mandy was holding. Lucy, smiling, turned to greet them, but the smile quickly froze as she noticed their concerned expressions.

'Oh! I see you've found out,' she said.

'Did you produce a duplicate?' blurted out Megan.

Lucy could see they were both in a high state of excitement and ignored the outburst. She tapped Mandy lightly on the bottom, 'Go and see your Mummy' she said.

'Aw! But it's not finished Lucy,' she wailed.

'Sorry,' said Lucy, 'we'll finish it later.'

'Promise?' she cried as she scampered out of the room.

'Promise,' echoed Lucy.

Jack moved into the room and sat down on the bed, 'How did you hear?' he inquired cautiously.

'I've been in the other dimension,' replied Lucy.

'You've got the laptop working then?'

She nodded.

Megan could feel the conversation was stilted, as if Lucy did not want to talk about her investigations. She suppressed her desire to demand an explanation from Lucy and left it to Jack to discover what he could.

'What did you make of the murder?' Jack persisted.

'I really don't know,' said Lucy, 'maybe I'm looking in the wrong places, but I can't see why this entity, whatever it is, would want to make a copy of me then kill it.'

'It was a copy of you then?'

'Oh yes, in every detail. I watched the autopsy; it's very scary when you're confronted with your own corpse, sort of a dead ringer. It's helped me of course, because the police are no longer looking for me, but I don't have any answers,' she said.

'Look at this' said Jack, handing her Megan's art book. Lucy glanced through the book while Jack and Megan watched intently for her reaction. As she looked at the pictures, her face began to register horror and disgust.

'You think it's this artist who's responsible for the demons?'

He nodded, 'I think he's managed in some way to use the portal, and may be feeding off your knowledge for his own purposes. What we don't know is what his intentions are.'

'One other thing,' interrupted Megan, unable to stay silent any longer, 'we can't be sure that you are not the copy and the real Lucy is lying in the morgue.'

There was a long leaden silence, Jack could feel the tension mounting and groaned inwardly. Megan thought Lucy looked uncomfortable as she struggled to understand their concern.

Suddenly she flung the book on the floor, 'You think I'm a stooge of this . . . thing? I trust you both with my work, with my life, let you into a most secret thing, and this is the loyalty you give me?' Shaking with rage, she turned to the small cupboard beside the bed, pulled out her few belongings and stuffed them into her hold all.

'What are you doing,' gasped Megan.

'I'm going to find this artist and give him piece of mind,' she spat out.

'What shall I tell Mandy?'

'You obviously don't trust me with Mandy. Tell her I'm sorry I couldn't stay to finish the jigsaw.' She flung open the door, ran downstairs and out of the house, leaving Jack and Megan staring at each other helplessly.

Jack flopped onto the vacated bed with a sigh. 'Well done!' he said resignedly. He gazed at the ceiling, trying to gather his thoughts, as a familiar smell from the pillow stimulated his nose. 'Carbolic! Of course she's the real Lucy' he exclaimed.

Megan stared at him in astonishment, 'so that's what that smell is.'

'We have to apologise to her for doubting her' said Jack.

. . . .

Lucy reasoned correctly that the police would no longer be interested in the house, as it was just an embarrassment to them now. It belonged to her father, and although he had been deported, he still had the right of ownership until it was sold. Her father, needless to say, was not going to sell it while he knew that Lucy was still living in it. Moving softly through the garden she retrieved the key and was soon sitting in front of her computer sending a coded email to her father. While she waited for him to respond she went over the events of the previous day in the hope of finding some clues which could help her understand the behaviour of whoever was controlling the demons. If it was this artist, Bosch, as Megan and Jack thought, what could he possibly gain by hatching this complicated plot, why was he protecting her, and for what nefarious purpose? She couldn't reach any conclusions and was hoping her father could help. However one thing of which she was acutely aware was that all this was preventing further experiments being carried out.

Suddenly her father's face appeared on her screen. After their usual greeting, Lucy quickly explained what had happened. 'What I can't understand Father, is why this Bosch person is doing this, I mean protecting and helping me.'

'You can be sure if his character is as you describe, then he's doing it to get something in return,' said Chu, 'and it's sure to be something you don't agree with; or he would ask directly.'

'What do you think I should do?' said Lucy.

'You must challenge him, but do so in the other dimension, there he cannot harm physically and your Buddhist training will protect you spiritually.'

'Can you explain Father, how this entity can produce a duplicate of me?'

'At the time he was alive, people did alchemy in Europe; and in China. They came close to understanding some of nature's secrets. They did not do experiments as we do, in a scientific way, so the results were . . . ah . . . inconsistent. Nevertheless, it is possible that some powers were identified, but un-useable without modern technology to manipulate them correctly. It is possible Mr. Bosch was . . . ah . . . alchemist and has seen the technology used by you to access the other dimension. He will preserve you for his own purpose. Wizards in The Middle Ages required a talisman to cast a spell; a lock of hair or fingernail clippings, without realizing that such things contained human D.N.A. He used the demons to bite you to get blood, and thereby D.N.A. information. He then has instructions to produce . . . ah . . . a duplicate of you.'

'It wouldn't be a duplicate though, would it Father?'

'Only the physical part; it would not have consciousness. But for a dead person, Mr. Bosch would not need consciousness. He could use a demon as a . . . ah . . . template. Be careful with this entity Lucy, he is clever, with nothing to lose. Don't be hard on your friends, they are concerned for you. Remember, you rely on each other from now on.'

For some time she sat in front of the blank computer screen, deliberately thinking through her next actions. Finally she reached forward and loaded the DVD into the machine.

CHAPTER 16

D I LIVINGSTONE EMERGED from Smiley's office wreathed in smiles and swung down the corridor with a jaunty air, as though a weight had been lifted from his shoulders, which indeed it had. The boss had insisted that the investigation required more "specialised officers", as she had put it, and although she realised that this would be, "an intense disappointment", he would have to pass up the challenge of solving this uniquely difficult case.

She has a fine way with words he thought as he swaggered into his office. He greeted Collins with a hearty, 'You can relax it's off, no more stressing your single brain cell.'

'What's happened?' he enquired.

'I think they've put the boffins onto it,' chortled Livingstone as he sank down into his welcoming chair, kicked off his shoes and swung his feet up onto the desk. Collins screwed up his nose.

'That's a shame,' he said. Livingstone looked at him quizzically. 'I've just had Johnson on the phone again. He reckons the D.N.A. of that body is not the same as the D.N.A. of the girl.'

'I really don't want to hear this, we are off the case,' said Livingstone emphatically.

'Well, yes I know, but it's interesting all the same,' he said, 'it's not even the D.N.A. of any known animal.'

'I have no further interest, I am not listening.'

'If you recall, we had the same sort of results after that business in the classroom. Do you think the two things are connected?'

'Will you please shut up and forget about it, that's an order!' growled Livingstone, but he knew that neither of them could.

. . . .

Lucy was about to give up when she sensed a presence in the void. She had spent some time thinking about the demons, but with no result. She tried to remember the face in the portal but that was a very weak image as, at the time it had appeared, she had been otherwise occupied. Of course, just because there was another entity in her mind didn't mean it was the one she wanted to contact.

Suddenly without warning her mind was filled with the screaming and wailing of a thousand devils swirling in a kaleidoscope of brilliant, dazzling, flashing, multi-coloured lights. Grotesque faces, snarling and leering, thrust themselves at her unrelentingly. Her natural instinct was to reel back from this ordeal, but experience told her that this could do no harm, so she held her nerve until the onslaught abated.

She formed the words, 'When you've quite finished your infantile ego trip, maybe we can talk.' The demons disappeared as quickly as they had come and there was silence for what seemed like an eternity, during which, she felt his presence around her, examining every corner of her personality.

'Well, well! You are a spirited little filly.'

The whisper was like a soft warm breeze on a balmy summer afternoon caressing her cheek. She remained impassive, her rigorous Buddhist training ensuring that she would not be seduced by such an approach.

'It is a real pleasure to talk with someone in your world after all this time, particularly someone as attractive as you. You are such a good upstanding person; you are good aren't you?'

She was irritated by this artificial conversation and could endure it no longer, 'Who are you and what do you want?' she threw at him bluntly.

'Patience, we have barely met. Our relationship is very special, I assure you there is no other like it in this part of the universe. We must nurture it gently like a delicate flower which will one day bloom in all its magnificence. Are you religious?'

'Why do you want to know?'

There was a short pause and then the response entered her mind, 'I need to know if you are a God fearing person, a good person. Only a good person can help me.'

'What have I to fear from God?'

There was a muffled expression of suppressed impatience.

Lucy continued, 'What is good . . . ? Who is to judge . . . ? Why . . . should I help you?'

There was another, more prolonged, silence.

'Who are you?' Lucy repeated, 'Why are you persecuting me and my friends?'

'Oh! My dear, you have more questions than the Inquisition, I had to get your attention, as your police have already discovered; you are a difficult person to find.'

'Why did you save me from the police?'

'There is something I want you to do for me, something that will benefit mankind in general and me in particular. I had to make sure you were not detained by the police. You would be of little value to me while in their custody.'

As he was transferring these thoughts an image began to take shape in her mind. Her first impression was of a hooded figure facing away from her. Slowly the head turned around to face her.

She was presented with a broad forehead and a heavy, sloping, overhanging brow. The eyes beneath it were deep set, glistening black in the shadows, slightly too close together and peering down either side of a long pointed nose. The chin was stubborn, while the mouth was a long cruel slit. Wisps of reddish hair could be seen spreading from the inside of the cowl otherwise the face was completely clean-shaven.

'You *should* help me if you are a good person.'

The apparition spoke but the lips did not move lending an unnerving strangeness to the conversation. It adopted what was intended to be a smile but looked more like a leer as Jerome continued to ingratiate himself with her. She concentrated hard on the face. It appeared as in a puppet show, as though someone was operating it remotely. There were no smooth transitions between its emotional states as there would be with a normal face. If this was really Jerome then Lucy had the feeling that he was being manipulated. She decided to irritate him.

'Should I recognise you?' thought Lucy antagonistically. 'Why would I even think you could be important enough to influence mankind's well being?'

The face became contorted and began to shake with rage, 'You are impudent and disrespectful,' he boomed.

'Ah! Now you show your real self to me,' was her response, 'you are an irrelevance, no one of any importance, who must have his own way regardless of who is hurt in the process. A petulant child stamping his foot demanding others look up to him with respect and punishing those who do not. You are someone who would gladly torture and kill to boost your own already over inflated self esteem. But you are not someone willing to reveal his true identity to me.'

Lucy was about to go on with the vilification, but the apparition had had enough.

'Quiet! You insolent little slut!' he screamed, 'I have never hurt anyone during, or after life.'

She had deliberately provoked him into a state of boiling anger where he was more vulnerable, suspecting she would learn more than if she had allowed him to conduct the conversation in his way.

'Who are you?' she repeated forcefully.

The hooded figure seemed to rise to its full height and with an effort controlled his rage, 'I am Jerome Van Aken,' he thundered, 'famous artist who was commissioned by no less than Philip the Second, King of Spain, to paint for him. I was, and still am, talented in ways you would not even begin to understand.'

Lucy kept the pressure up, 'If you're so darned clever, why do you need an "insolent little slut" like me?'

Jerome was quiet for a while as he began to realise why Lucy was needling him.

'It is true, you could be of use to me,' he conceded, his anger abating, 'and you would be handsomely rewarded should you choose to assist me. However if you have no desire to bargain I will in time undoubtedly find another way, and in this accursed place the one thing I have is time.'

'You can offer me nothing I don't already have,' replied Lucy.

'Then there is no more to be said.'

Lucy sensed that she had perhaps pushed him too far, although, she reasoned, she had to establish that he could not expect to dominate her, and so her approach was justifiable. She decided to bring him back from the edge by appealing to his vanity.

'Your paintings are much admired, what was their purpose?'

There was another silence as Jerome considered Lucy's reasons for her sudden change of direction. Finally he could resist the temptation for self aggrandisement no longer.

'I was described as a stern moralist,' he began, 'and so I was. My mission on earth was one of enlightenment; of educating the lubberts to understand that if they continued with their corruption and sinful behaviour they would inevitably be cast into purgatory when they died. This I did using the medium of paint as that was the only way to achieve the audience I desired. The society you and your kind have built since my death makes it even more urgent that I continue my work. Since I now have knowledge of purgatory I am the ideal person to help society regain its moral structure, you must help me to help society. I have watched, in this last five hundred years, the decline of goodness and the upsurge of sin, now I must act before it's too late. With your help and your modern communications I know I can achieve great things. We can achieve great things!'

'So what are you proposing, a second coming?' she enquired sarcastically.

'I should be released from this infernal purgatory to fulfil my great promise.'

'Ah!' cried Lucy, 'So your sins placed you into purgatory. They must have been quite something, and you want me to help you to live again so that you can sin again? Other people in your situation elect to follow the spiritual direction and better themselves, in order to make them worthy of future physical lives, that is the natural law, why do you not follow this path?'

'I see you have some knowledge of the occult,' he replied.

'I am a Buddhist,' she said, 'but you are avoiding the question.'

'I had no choice, there was a misunderstanding,' he said abruptly.

'Your actions determine choice,' countered Lucy, 'it is a built in function of the oneness of everything. It is Karmic law.'

'Don't try to confuse me with your fuddled eastern mysticism, the subject is closed,' spat back Jerome.

'OK, I shall then draw my own conclusions about your motivation.'

'So be it.'

'In life you strayed from the right path and now you're being punished in self imposed purgatory, I am right aren't I?'

'This subject is not for discussion,' snapped Jerome.

'I get the picture now,' continued Lucy, 'you know that through my work, I can transfer consciousness between dimensions. What you expect me to do, is release you from purgatory, reconnect your personality with physical matter in the material world and release you from the frustration of been a physical personality in a spiritual world. All this about wanting to help society is rubbish; you are a hypocrite and a lying hypocrite at that. Why should I help you? You are the architect of your own disaster and if I were to help you, you would simply create more disasters.'

Jerome was silent. Lucy knew she had hit the mark and that he was now considering his options. As she watched, the area behind the face began to grow darker, as though a shadow had been cast on it. The face twitched spasmodically, shuddered and finally assumed an expression of abject horror. The shadow slowly enveloped and obscured the terrified face. Lucy thought she sensed the word "master", and then there was nothing.

There followed a long pause. Just as she was about to give up he burst into her consciousness again, 'I will prove that my imprisonment was unjustified, that I am not guilty of the crimes of which I was accused. I will show that I am no more evil than anybody else who found himself in the same circumstances as I. I will show this, and you will help me because you are a good person. You will help me, or I will create hell on earth.'

'You can only frighten people in your present state,' said Lucy, suddenly alarmed.

'You forget, my dear,' he intoned in sinister fashion, 'although I cannot materialise myself, I can materialise my little friends.'

CHAPTER 17

M EGAN AND JACK went to school the next day having decided that they should call on Lucy after school to apologise for mistrusting her. Megan was still suspicious that Lucy may have been substituted, but as Lucy was no longer in her house she thought any immediate danger was now past.

Throughout the day strange stories circulated around the school, which made Megan feel more relaxed about Lucy. They suggested that the body discovered on the playing field was not even human, something which intrigued the rest of the school but came as no surprise to Megan and Jack.

It was shortly after lunch that events overtook Megan's good intentions with regard to Lucy in the bulky form of DI Livingstone. He appeared at the library door along with Chalky White who motioned for her to join them. Megan, who had been talking to Jack, crossed the library apprehensively.

'I'm afraid I have some bad news,' said Livingstone after introducing himself, 'your sister has disappeared and we are afraid she may have been abducted.'

Megan stared at Livingstone, her pretty face frozen in shocked horror. She swayed slightly, Chalky put out a hand to steady her. He glanced across at Jack who was watching intently.

'M . . . Mandy?' stammered Megan, 'You must be mistaken, who would want to do a thing like that?'

'At the moment we have no idea Miss, but I'm afraid it's true; your parents are in shock and terribly distressed. We feel that you should go home to give them what support you can.'

'Come on,' said Chalky gently, 'I'd better take you home.' She nodded numbly as he took her elbow and guided her out of the library.

As they approached her house, Rosie appeared at the door. Her tear stained face was bloated and flushed, while Bobbie hovered in the background muttering viscous threats against the unseen enemy.

Megan introduced Chalky to her parents then disappeared indoors with her mother. Bobbie eyed the teacher suspiciously.

'You 'er teacher then?' he grunted.

'Yes,' replied Chalky, 'do you know what happened?'

'She was playing in the garden mister, God 'elp the sod if I get 'old of 'im.' This was emphasised by one massive fist crashing into the palm of the other.

'Can I see the garden?' enquired Chalky.

Bobbie squeezed through the narrow alleyway into the garden with Chalky following.

Chalky stopped at the ramshackle gate and rested his hand on what remained of the gate post. He felt a sticky substance adhering to the post and raising his fingers up to his nose, sniffed. Bobbie uncomprehendingly looked on as Chalky pulled a handkerchief from his pocket and rubbed vigorously at the post. Policemen doing a fingertip search of the pasture grass in the small garden continued their activities unaware.

'Mm,' said Chalky to himself, 'how odd.'

Bobbie scratched his head, 'I've got friends,' he said menacingly, 'we'll find the bastard, and when we do . . . '

Chalky looked at the distressed giant, 'I think you'd better leave this to the police,' he said through pursed lips and quickly left.

Jack had more or less got the gist of what had happened and decided to skip the afternoon lessons and go straight around to Lucy's house.

'Where's your suspicious girlfriend?' said Lucy as she greeted him at the conservatory door.

Jack motioned her inside, 'She was going to apologise for mistrusting you, but she's had to go home.' He quickly explained to the horrified Lucy what had happened. Briefly she filled Jack in with the events of the previous evening and the parting threat from Jerome.

Jack gasped, 'You think Jerome has kidnapped Mandy to force you to do his dirty work?'

'I'm afraid so.'

'What are we going to do?' asked Jack.

'The first thing we have to do, is make sure that she hasn't been harmed in any way.'

'How can you do that? You don't even know where she's been kept.'

'No but I have a good idea who's keeping her. Anyway, while I was looking after her, I recorded her quantum fingerprint. I'll load it onto the computer and then try to locate her.'

'OK, what then?' said Jack.

'Then I have to find out what our egotistical bully boy wants from me?'

They made their way upstairs to the computer room and Lucy loaded the DVD containing Mandy's information and opened the portal. Jack watched the screen intently waiting for any instructions as Lucy went back to the conservatory. She established herself in the other dimension quickly, and then concentrated hard on Mandy's image. Almost immediately she was presented with the picture of the child's lifeless body lying in a copse on a layer of bracken. Two demons were close by, grinning evilly. She recoiled with shock, then quickly realised that if Jerome had killed the child he would have nothing with which to bargain.

There was a short pause then Jerome infiltrated her mind, 'Do you like my little preview?' he said scornfully, 'You see I can place her wherever I like in whatever state I choose, so any attempt at rescue is futile.'

'You depraved lunatic,' snapped Lucy, 'I'm not surprised you had a "misunderstanding" as you call it.'

Jerome adopted a mocking, threatening tone, leaving no doubt of the seriousness of his intent. 'Now that's no way to get the little girl back safe. It's of no consequence to me whether she lives or dies and I think it would serve you well to remember that.'

She hesitated, 'OK, what is it you want from me?'

'That's better Lucy, now we are partners, I can call you Lucy can't I?' he said.

She shuddered at the proposed intimacy. '*As long as I can call you slimeball*', she thought inadvertently.

'What is a slimeball?'

'Never mind, what do you want?'

'I need a sample of what you call D.N.A.,' he said, 'my D.N.A. with which you will release me from purgatory.'

Lucy groaned inwardly, this is what she had been afraid of. With her technology and his D.N.A., it was his passport to renewed life in the third dimension!

'What you are proposing is impossible,' she protested.

'You are lying; I have been watching your activities for some time and I know it's possible. Please remember what's at stake.' With the threat returned the impression of the child but this time with her head just above the rim of a giant cooking pot which was sitting on a blazing fire, guarded by a leering devil holding a saw. She knew then there was no other way to save Mandy.

'OK, where can I get it from?'

'From s'Hertogenbosch, in the Netherlands of course,' he replied.

Lucy was stunned, how could she retrieve tissue from a grave somewhere in Holland?

'How can I trust you to return her unharmed, I don't even know if she's alive at this moment?'

'I'll show her to you.'

'That won't prove anything; you've already shown you can manipulate her image in any way you choose.'

Jerome was temporarily unsure, he knew Lucy would only co-operate if she was confident Mandy was unharmed, and because of his initial boasting she would no longer believe anything he showed her. After a long pause he replied, 'Very well, I will return her to you, but remember no one can stop me getting her back whenever I choose. You have two days in which to retrieve the D.N.A., if you do not succeed I will surely kill her, and many others, until you do.'

From his tone Lucy knew he meant business and after all, what did he have to lose? She was the only person who could help him achieve his ambition. She could hold out against him of course, but then, that could lead to a trail of bodies before, eventually, she would have to succumb to his evil plan.

'Where's this grave you want me to rob?'

'Oh! My dear I wouldn't dream of subjecting you to anything so unladylike,' he mocked, 'you merely have to retrieve a lock of my hair.'

'Well that shouldn't be difficult to find.'

Jerome ignored the sarcasm, 'The hair is in a bible which I presented to my wife as a wedding gift. It is one of the first printed bibles and is in the Zwanenbroederstraat Museum on 94 Hinthamersraat.'

The precision with which this was stated took Lucy by surprise, and so she had to ask him to repeat it before she could commit it to memory.

'When I have the hair,' she said, 'what then?'

'You then have to breathe new life into me.'

'How do you suppose you will fit into modern society?'

'Do not think I have been idle for the last five hundred years. I have worked out my plans.'

'Which are?'

'You think you can trick me? You have two days,' he snarled and then, he was gone.

Lucy and Jack discussed their plans until it was time for Jack to return home and pretend he had been at school in the afternoon. On his way he called at Megan's house, as he and Lucy had agreed, to find that Mandy had indeed been found, and although smelling disgustingly and telling strange stories of bogeymen, she was no worse for wear.

Megan had informed the police, who were now confused as to the motive for the abduction and the circumstances of her return. Jack suggested they regroup at Lucy's house later and went home to send an email to Lucy confirming Mandy's return.

CHAPTER 18

'I CAN'T DO this on my own,' insisted Lucy.

'You're right of course,' replied Jack, 'I'll have to go with you.'

'Will it mean an overnight stay in Holland?' asked Megan suspiciously.

'Probably,' said Lucy, 'why?'

'I'll come with you, all three of us could go together,' suggested Megan hopefully.

Jack looked at Lucy; he assumed that she wouldn't want any jealous undercurrent affecting her concentration so he cut in, 'I think with today's events, the last thing your parents want is another daughter to disappear. You need to keep a watchful eye on Mandy as you will be the only person who is aware of the danger she's in.' Lucy emphatically nodded her agreement.

'Well, I suppose so,' agreed Megan reluctantly.

It was arranged that Jack would tell his parents that he would be sleeping over at a friend's house the following evening in order that they could do some troublesome homework together. He would appear to be going to school as normal in the morning. Megan would cover for his absence by ticking his name in the class register. This would not be difficult as Chalky didn't seem particularly interested in the administrative side of teaching and often didn't bother with the register at all.

. . . .

All went according to plan and by mid morning Jack and Lucy were sitting together on the flight from Heathrow to Schipol, Amsterdam. Jack thanked his lucky stars that he had got his own passport only last summer. He felt a surge of excitement as the aircraft soared into the steely blue, early morning sky. Although he could easily justify his actions he knew that if his parents could see him now they would be livid. The fact that he was doing this without their knowledge or assistance added an extra thrill to the adventure. He squared his shoulders against the back of the seat and told himself he was capable of doing anything that was required of him.

Lucy glanced sideways at him. As though realising he had overcome an internal struggle, she laid her small soft hand on his and squeezed gently.

'You OK?' she said.

'Sure!' he replied, and he meant it.

For a while she gave him some insight into the manipulation of the algorithms involved in generating the portal.

'How come nobody has ever discovered this before?' he inquired.

'The problem is perception and blind alleys. It's very easy to allow yourself to believe you are making progress when in fact you are not. It's like when you are playing football; take your eye off the ball and you're lost. When you investigate this subject from the higher dimensions it's obvious where you've been going wrong but you have to get there first, that's the difficult bit. Even Einstein convinced himself that his approach was right, only to be proven wrong in time. Had he been able to view the quantum world from the standpoint of other dimensions, he would have been able to grasp the overall picture with much better clarity. Everything is simpler when viewed from the higher dimensions. When you were in the other dimension I expect you had the impression of fields of different coloured vibrations with varying densities.'

'Yes, that's right,' he agreed.

'What you felt was the physical objects in this world as they are in the higher dimension, which is as vibrations of pure energy at different frequencies. There are no particles as such, which is how we describe it in this dimension with all its complications of size, spin, velocity, distance, molecular structure and so on. There is only energy vibrating at different frequencies, only one variable; that's what makes it so much easier to handle.'

'Let me just get my head around this,' said Jack, 'are you saying that messing around at the atomic level is unnecessary?'

'No, what I mean is that if you ignore other possibilities while you're doing that and don't look at the bigger picture, you may miss the key to it all.'

'And that's what scientists have been doing up to now?'

'Possibly, I can't say for sure but I do know it doesn't help when you allow yourself to be misled.'

'Do you think science has been led down the wrong road?'

'I think that happens all the time and it's not helped by institutions protecting their own interests while influencing the scientific community and stifling innovation.'

'But I thought researchers were supposed to be investigating new ideas,' protested Jack.

'They are normally only allowed to do that where it fits in with the politics of their superiors.'

He decided not to pursue that discussion any further as Lucy obviously had very fixed views on the academic and political structures in England, possibly formed out of the frustrations encountered by her father.

. . . .

'All I know,' complained Livingstone, 'is that the more I try to shake off this damned thing, the more it comes back to haunt me.'

Collins nodded sympathetically.

'I just don't know what to make of this report,' sighed Livingstone, 'seen boarding a plane for Holland this morning. The other day, she was dead with a rat in her stomach, today she's going Dutch with a boyfriend, and we have instructions to do nothing about it. What the hell is going on?' He turned to Collins appealingly, who was trying to make himself as small as possible.

'You have to admire the lads at Heathrow for spotting her in the first place,' he said, trying to divert the conversation.

'I wish they hadn't,' groaned Livingstone, 'I would have been quite happy to forget the whole thing.'

'What about the boy, who is he?'

'Ah! Well, for once that's straightforward enough. His name is Jack Dawkins, or at least that's the name in his passport and he lives locally.'

'Maybe we should pay his parents a visit and ask them if they know where their son is?' suggested Collins.

'That's not a bad idea,' agreed Livingstone, 'except we have been instructed not to interfere by the boss.'

'Easy to say and difficult to do, particularly when it's happening on our patch,' said Collins, sensing some action.

'My patch, if you don't mind.'

Collins wilted under the rebuke, his confidence had not yet returned after his ordeal with Jerome's demons and he was now widely regarded by his colleagues as a wimp who was unable to deal with a seven-stone girl. Livingstone circled his desk several times, 'If I don't get to the bottom of this it will haunt me for the rest of my life,' he muttered.

'Perhaps we could treat it as an unrelated enquiry,' said Collins in a small voice.

'What do you mean?'

'What about playing truant from school?'

'Why would a senior police officer be interested in truancy?' said Livingstone.

'Well, you wouldn't be, but you would if drug running was involved.'

Livingstone stopped marching around his desk and looked at Collins, his mouth sagging open and his bleary eyes half closed.

'I suppose he is going to Amsterdam, probably without his parent's permission. Who knows what they intend to get up to there.' Livingstone's heavy jowls began to wobble.

'What about the abduction of the little girl?' said Collins.

'Mm, something's very odd there as well. The whole thing must be connected in some way. We have the incident at the school, the girl, abducted then not abducted, her sister in the same class as this Dawkins lad, and then the

Chinese girl who was dead and is no more. Could all that be coincidental?'

Livingstone continued to march around the desk, his frown deepened. Collins slumping further into his chair remarked, 'At least we know we can nab them as they return to Heathrow and clear up the whole thing then.'

Livingstone's face became taut with the expectation, 'Yes there is that,' he said slowly.

. . . .

Jack stopped in front of the ticket machine, 'I can't even understand the English instructions,' he said despairingly. Lucy slipped in-between him and the machine, fed coins into it, and pressed buttons at lightning speed.

'There,' she said as the tickets obediently rolled out, 'did you get that?'

His handsome features screwed into disbelief, 'You've done this before,' he ventured.

She grinned mischievously, 'It's not a problem for a normal person,' she said. 'Do you think you could find the platform?'

Ignoring her scorn he looked around the railway station forecourt. It was busy with the chaotic buzz of multinational activity. A slice of humanity all going goodness knows where for whatever reason, and he was confused. The excitement he had earlier felt on the plane returned as he realised that he was part of this, he could join in and make a contribution. Indeed the contribution he could make was unique. Suddenly feeling confident he took hold of her hand. 'Come on! Let's go and get it; platform six I think!' With that he strode purposefully into the atrium. Lucy giggled and examined his now composed and determined face.

'You'll do,' she said affectionately, and clipped him on the chin with her small fist.

. . . .

'So, what do you make of it all; Jerome I mean?' said Jack later.

Lucy stretched, yawned and looked out of the window as the flat Dutch countryside rolled by. The train from Schipol to Amsterdam had only taken twenty minutes and the connection to Den Bosch, as the Dutch called it, was spot on time. They should be at their destination in less than an hour.

'They have quaint houses don't they,' she said admiringly as they passed by a small village with its sugar loaf houses and thatched roof cottages.

'It's lovely,' he agreed, 'but what about Jerome?' he said waving his hand at Megan's art book lying on the table between them. She picked it up and flicked through the pages of paintings until she reached the part describing the little which was known about Hieronymous Bosch.

'It says here that he was a deeply religious man who used his art to warn people about the dangers of sin.'

'Go on.'

Lucy screwed up her face in an expression of disgust, 'Having sampled his smelly demons and the damage they can do, I would say he is not a particularly charitable Christian.'

Jack glanced at her seated cross-legged opposite him. The fresh wounds were clearly visible where the cut off jeans did not cover her legs. He shuddered involuntarily at the memory of the demons.'His paintings are pornographic by our standards, so five hundred years ago they must have been dynamite,' he said.

'He told me that the King of Spain collected his paintings, it confirms that here,' she said, pointing at the descriptive text.

'Sort of nudge, nudge . . . want to buy a dirty picture?'

'He justified his art by claiming he was guiding people away from the inevitable consequences of their self indulgence. He wanted me to help him continue with his work.'

'Well he may have *thought* he was helping, but was he just peddling titillation?'

She ignored the question, grinned wickedly and pretended to gaze soulfully into his eyes, 'I shouldn't think you need any help of that sort do you Jack?'

He blushed and took refuge in the view outside the train window.

'Sorry, couldn't resist it,' she said apologetically.

After a strained silence, he finally recovered from his embarrassment, 'Are you religious Lucy?'

Startled by the question it was now Lucy's turn to examine the view. Finally she answered, 'Well I suppose it depends what you mean by religious.' She turned to face him, 'My father is a Buddhist, and he brought me up with those beliefs. My mother is a Catholic, so there was plenty of scope for misunderstanding there. Since then, and mainly because of the results of our work, I have become more inclined towards a Taoist understanding of reality. This accepts the interconnectedness of everything as a matter of scientific fact. Everything that happens, even your thoughts, has an effect elsewhere, borne out by our experiments with quantum entanglement which proves that these relationships can be transmitted over vast distances. So I believe science and religion do not have to be in conflict, all that's required is a shift in our perception for them to be in agreement.'

None of this made any sense to Jack. Obviously he had had some instruction in school about other religions but it was usually presented as science and religion being at odds with each other. The concepts proposed by Lucy were alien to him.

'You are saying that religion and science are connected?'

'Of course they are! They are part of the same whole,' she said firmly. 'You've experienced the much simplified view of our third dimension from other dimensions. The complexity of this dimension disappears when viewed from that perspective and you can then see that everything is part of the same whole. The only reason for matter being present in our dimension is the different frequencies of operation of atoms involved. They are, if you like, condensed spots of energy in an overall energy field.'

'So what's that got to do with this Tao thing?'

'The Eastern sages were teaching that principle two and a half thousand years ago. Tao means oneness. In other words, everything is related to everything else. Good and bad are opposites of the same thing. What Tao does is to maintain the balance between them. This is represented by the symbol of Yin and Yang.'

'Oh yes, I've seen that somewhere before,' interrupted Jack, relieved to be able to make some sort of contribution. 'That's the split circle with two dots in it.'

'Yes that's it.'

He gazed thoughtfully out of the window at the grey sky mottled with darker grey blobs of more intense cloud. The experience of his mind being alone in a void returned and he visualised the clouds as clumps of matter in a chaotic, ever changing energy field, areas of stability necessary to establish third dimensional materiality.

'So how does this apply to our poor misguided friend?'

Lucy looked at the book again, 'It says here that his wife was associated through her family with the Catholic Church and she was quite well off.'

'No struggling artist then, he wouldn't need to paint for a living.'

'No, but for obvious reasons he would have to fall in line with the church, which was all powerful at that time. You'd have thought that he'd have painted typical religious themes, but he was obviously driven to produce pornography for the ruling classes, whereas he's claiming he produced it to educate the masses.'

'I think he was in torment while he was alive, his problem was justifying the contradiction to himself,' said Jack.

'He may have been an alchemist,' she said, closing the book and returning to the view.

'What's that?'

'They were a sect of people, wizards if you like, who claimed all sorts of special powers over nature.'

'What powers did they have?'

'Well for one thing they claimed they could turn base metal into gold.'

He whistled softly through his teeth, 'Wow! Some trick, and could they?'

'Who knows?' said Lucy, 'Certainly we can, if we wanted to.'

This came like a thunderbolt to Jack, 'You mean we . . . , you . . . , could be rich overnight?'

'Of course,' she said in a matter of fact fashion.

Jack felt his mouth go dry, 'So why don't you?' he croaked.

'I don't have any ambition to be rich, nor do you, in spite of your interest. I picked you for your morals, not your greed. I know that you can resist that sort of temptation.'

Jack was struggling with his thoughts when suddenly he recalled his conversation with Dipper, "money's the problem, not the solution", he had said.

He slumped back in his seat and took a deep breath. He felt like a child whose ice cream had fallen from the top of his cone and rolled into the gutter. He realised she was, as with most things, absolutely right. It was not in his nature to seek out wealth.

'Witch!' he murmured.

Lucy turned from the window, 'Look on the bright side, at least you've got me as a friend,' she said, with an engaging smile.

He looked at her and his heart skipped a couple of beats, 'I didn't want the rotten ice cream anyway,' he said.

'What ice cream?'

'Never mind, it wasn't important.'

CHAPTER 19

MEGAN LOOKED UP at the wall clock, *they should be there by now*, she thought. Chalky was writing on the board with his back to the class and didn't see Collins' face appear at the window in the classroom door. Megan recognised him at once, *what does he want?* she thought anxiously, *maybe something's gone wrong.*

Collins entered the room tentatively and motioned to Chalky, who moved over to speak with him. In spite of their hushed tones she picked up the gist of their conversation and sure enough it was about Jack. To her amazement she distinctly heard Chalky say, 'I've sent him off on an errand at the other side of the school; yes he's here, I marked him off in the register myself this morning.'

Her mind was in turmoil, *why is Chalky providing an alibi for Jack? Unless of course he doesn't know where Jack is and is just trying to get rid of Collins as quickly as possible.* As if the astonished expression on Megan's face had prompted him, Chalky could quite clearly be heard to say, 'I'd rather you didn't disturb my class if you don't mind.'

Collins looked confused, how could this be? He made to turn to the class but as if anticipating his actions Chalky headed him off with, 'Could you please close the door on your way out?' Collins left as timorously as he had entered.

As the class finished, Dipper appeared at Megan's side, 'What was all that about? Where is Jack anyway? Why do you suppose Chalky's covering up for him?' he said.

'How would I know?' she said, quickening her pace as they walked along the corridor.

'I thought you had special powers,' insisted Dipper, 'as you're in league with,' he inclined his eyes upwards, 'the other side.'

'What do you mean?'

'That poltergeist, you caused it didn't you? You were absolutely still while the classroom was being wrecked, completely unnatural if you ask me.'

'Well I'm not asking you, see.'

Dipper attempted to keep up with her as they hurried down the corridor, narrowly avoiding contact with pupils coming in the opposite direction. Finally he managed to overtake and confront her, 'Aw! Come on Megan you can tell me what's going on, I'm Jack's best friend,' he said, spreading his hands appealingly.

'I don't know what you're talking about boyo, and by the way, I don't agree with everything Jack does, that includes his choice of dodgy, podgy, friends,' she said and pushed him roughly out of the way.

Dipper's round eyes followed her down the corridor, 'There's definitely something very odd going on here,' he muttered to himself, 'she's never called me 'boyo' before.'

He turned away thoughtfully, a mistake in the busiest corridor in the school as he was immediately trampled and buffeted by younger pupils streaming from their classrooms. For Dipper, this was becoming a challenge his nature could not ignore. He was determined to get to the bottom of the mystery.

. . . .

'Well?' said Livingstone, 'What's the story?'

'He's at school,' said Collins.

He fixed him with a stony glare and swung his legs off the desk.

'Then how do you explain his appearance at Heathrow this morning at the Amsterdam check in?'

'I . . . I can't,' stammered Collins.

'You berk!' yelled Livingstone, his face turning purple, 'I send you off to do a simple job, and you come back with half a story . . . the wrong half!'

Collins shuffled his feet sheepishly, 'Sorry boss,' he whispered.

Livingstone jumped to his feet and circled his desk a few times, intermittently touching the telephone as he went. Collins flinched at each prod of the stubby finger.

'I smell a rat,' growled Livingstone, 'a great, fat, ugly one.' He waved his hand in the vague direction of the Pathology lab, 'And it's not in that freak's stomach either.'

Suddenly he grabbed the phone and rattled out a number, causing Collins to jump nervously.

'Johnson? It's Livingstone; what else have you found with this er . . . er . . . body.'

'Oh nothing much,' said Johnson guardedly.

Suspecting he was hiding something Livingstone persisted, 'What does that mean?'

'Well, there's nothing more to say.'

'Spit it out Johnson, what have you found?'

Johnson's voice was uncharacteristically shaky; 'Nothing, absolutely nothing.'

'What's happened?'

'It's disappeared,' said Johnson meekly.

'Disappeared? Even you can't lose a whole cadaver.'

'I haven't lost it. Obviously it was kept locked up . . . it's just melted away, even the tissue samples have gone.'

Livingstone breathed heavily down the phone for a few seconds, trying to organise his thoughts.

'What about the rat?'

'Oh! That's still here.'

'Still here eh! I thought I could smell something,' muttered Livingstone.

Collins sniggered but was silenced by the dark look fired at him.

'When did this happen?' asked Livingstone.

'Sometime in the night.'

'Well you're the boffin, how did it happen?'

'I haven't a clue Ken.'

Livingstone knew when Johnson used his first name further enquiry was useless, and so he replaced the receiver and sank back into his chair with his head in his hands.

'Maybe we should just do what the boss told us to do' Collins said hopefully.

Livingstone grunted from beneath his hands, 'Yes, I know, forget it, we are no longer on the case,' he intoned. 'The trouble is I can't forget it. How's this young lad Dawkins got involved? I have an awful feeling that pretty soon a lot of people are going to get very hurt and we will be responsible for not stopping it.'

. . . .

Lucy smiled at Jack, 'Of course at that time the Renaissance was beginning to take hold in southern Europe, particularly in Italy,' she said.

'So why is that significant?'

'It must have caused tensions in this community, where the Catholic Church was a powerful force.'

He was puzzled, 'How do you know that?'

'An educated guess; check out the size of its Cathedral and the likely size of the town in the fifteenth century,' she pointed at a photograph in the book.

'Phew! I see what you mean. It says here that it's the biggest Cathedral in Holland. So you think there would have been a lot of resistance to the ideas and influences coming out of Italy?'

'Certainly!' replied Lucy, 'The Renaissance gave all people the opportunity to take responsibility for their own thoughts and deeds instead of offloading it onto a group of self elected individuals claiming to be representatives of God. That would have reduced their power over the townspeople and their ability to sell indulgences.'

'Right, I remember something about that from history, Martin Luther and all that,' said Jack.

'It was a good source of income for the Church. People were led to believe they were buying salvation. The Renaissance threatened to bypass all the middlemen who were living off the fears of the common people.'

'So that would have made Jerome uneasy?'

'I think Jerome had a foot in each camp. I suspect he was sympathetic to the new thinking, but didn't want to prejudice his comfortable lifestyle living off his wife's money and painting pornography for the hierarchy. He must have been aware that he was been dragged into the same trap as his patrons. Doing it in ignorance is forgivable, with full knowledge; he would eventually place himself into purgatory. He needs to find some way to forgive himself now.'

'So I think what you're saying is that he was basically a good person corrupted by those around him.'

'Yes I think his only crimes were his sensitivity and human weakness. The purgatory he expressed in his paintings was the anticipation of his own fate. Maybe by placing it on canvas he hoped to escape it and absolve his own sin, sort of relieve his conscience, it could have been his very public confessional. The Renaissance placed the blame for his actions fairly and squarely on his own shoulders, no more, "do as you like through the week" . . . three "Hail Marys" on Sunday and start over with a clean sheet on Monday. He was closer to the Church's hypocrisy than most, which must have heightened his concern. Once he embarked on the road to pleasing his sponsors, of course, he was caught in their trap and there was no way out. If he objected he could have been burnt at the stake as a heretic.'

'How do you explain his attitude now?'

'I can't. I do think though that there's more to this than we know so far. I keep remembering his face as that shadow crept over it. It was the face of absolute despair, as though he were haunted by some fearful thing.'

Jack sat silently watching the Brabant countryside rolling by, 'What's the Buddhist view of all this?'

'We each create our own salvation or hell,' she said, 'because of Karma.'

Jack looked at her stupidly for a moment, 'You mean sex, as in Sutra?'

'No! Idiot!' She glanced at her oversized watch; 'How long have we got?' she asked.

'Nearly twelve o'clock, we're almost there.'

'OK, it'll have to be a potted version. Whatever you think or do has an effect of some sort on your consciousness, and conditions your future actions and thoughts. This always results in repercussions as you interact with your environment, some good and maybe some bad. The Buddhist way teaches that the effects of these self-inflicted causes may not appear for many lifetimes. This can mean that someone who is apparently disadvantaged in their current lifetime may be paying off a debt from a previous one.'

He looked puzzled, 'So what's the point of it?'

'The point is that we all have to make a gradual progression away from material things and become more spiritually inclined, because that is a natural law for humans. The objective is to accumulate more good Karma with each successive life and break away from the shackles of material existence to reach enlightenment. Once that's achieved, there's no further reason for physical life because you will have understood everything that it can offer.'

'So when you've achieved enlightenment, you live exclusively in other dimensions, how many are there?'

'Nobody knows how many more there may be, at the last count, string theory predicted eleven.'

'String theory?' echoed Jack.

'We'll not go into that,' said Lucy, smiling at his consternation.

'Where did this Karma law come from, I mean who invented it?'

'It's a natural law, like evolution, it's inevitable and there is no escape from it. No one invented it, it grew with us as we evolved,' said Lucy.

'I think I see, so where does this leave poor old Jerome? He seems to have exactly the opposite ambitions to the ones he should.'

'Yes,' said Lucy thoughtfully, 'it doesn't seem to add up for a religious person does it? The point is that his condition is not as a result of an unsympathetic all controlling deity; it's his own deeds or thoughts that have led him into purgatory. Blaming God will only make it worse.'

The train began to slow down, 'So how does he get out of it?' queried Jack.

'He has to accept the reason for his situation and then begin to change the way he thinks.'

'If I understand you correctly, what we are going to do will only enable him to dig a deeper hole for himself.'

'At the moment I don't see that we have any alternative,' she said as she stepped onto the platform.

They had been so engrossed in their conversation that they failed to notice a short stocky man dressed in a blue duffel coat and black woollen hat, dismount at the same stop and follow them at a discreet distance out of the station.

They emerged from the railway station and crossed over the small bridge spanning the river Dommel. From where they stood they could easily see the great Gothic Cathedral dominating the town. The magnificent building soared heavenwards, a tribute to medieval craftsmen and man's ability to rise above mediocrity.

'I can see why the Church was so influential then,' remarked Jack, 'you could hardly miss it.'

'I'm starving,' said Lucy, 'let's head for the centre and have something to eat before we get our bearings.'

It was only a short step to the main square where they found several pavement cafes, their external frontages closed for the winter. They went into the nearest and sat down at a table by the window. Lucy looked around, the café was empty. She pulled aside the heavy net curtains and surveyed the deserted street.

'I like Holland, it's a shame about the weather,' she said as heavy raindrops began to splash against the glass. A middle aged, slightly bent waiter came across to their table wearing an amenable smile. As he took their order he noticed their art book lying on the table and engaged them in conversation.

'We don't get many tourists at this time of the year,' he said in perfect English.

'We're not tourists,' said Jack politely, 'we're doing research for a thesis.'

'You're doing research on this fellow?' he asked stabbing a finger at the book.

'Yes that's right,' agreed Lucy.

The waiter leaned forward conspiratorially, 'You know you won't find much about him, even here, where he was born and lived all his life.'

'Why is that?' asked Jack, his interest aroused.

'He wasn't much liked here, although he helps to bring some business,' he laughed. 'You will find his statue in front of the town hall, and if you like when you've finished your meal, I'll show you where he lived,' he said helpfully.

'That's very kind of you,' said Jack.

'All part of the service,' said the waiter, and disappeared into the kitchen.

'It seems as though they're not particularly proud of their famous son,' said Jack.

Lucy nodded, 'He's only one opinion among thousands but it's worth asking him why; the more information we can gather, the better.'

When the waiter came back with their lunch, he sat down at the table and chatted with them for a while. It was clear from his remarks that at some point in his life Jerome had been branded as a heretic by at least some of the population of Den Bosch.

'Was it his paintings that offended people?' asked Lucy.

'There were stories that he was a witch,' said the waiter mysteriously. He hunched forward, his nose barely a few inches above the book, as though to concentrate his thoughts. 'It was said that he was in league with the Devil, trying to undermine the church by selling the Devil's work to them.'

'It seems that he couldn't escape criticism whatever he did,' said Jack.

Lucy gave Jack a knowing look, 'A foot in each camp and could please neither,' she murmured.

The waiter looked at Lucy quizzically, 'People said he was a hypocrite; he preached abstinence but sinned himself.'

'I expect he passed his load of sin onto God on Sunday?' said Lucy.

'Everybody did then, and a lot still do,' replied the waiter. 'Excuse me!'

He moved to the other side of the room to take the order of the man wearing the duffel coat, who had just entered the café.

'What do you think?' said Jack.

'It all seems to fit,' she said through a mouthful of beef, 'then again you can't be sure of any story almost five hundred years old, particularly if told from prejudice.'

He leaned across the table and wiped a piece of beef from her chin.

'Your eating habits haven't improved much,' he grinned.

'I don't suppose your room is any tidier either,' she countered.

'Our relationship must be getting better, you didn't spit at me.'

'Perhaps, just don't count on it,' she laughed.

Later with their meal finished, the waiter took them over the road to the Town Hall where stood the bronze statue of Hieronymus Bosch. Lucy spent some time gazing up at it then carelessly remarked, 'It doesn't much look like him.'

The waiter turned to her with a puzzled look, 'How do you know this?' he said.

'Oh, I think I remember seeing a picture somewhere,' she said, flustered.

'You must be mistaken, there are no other pictures of this man,' said the waiter.

'You're right I am mistaken,' she agreed quickly.

The waiter led them down the Hinthamerstraat and pointed at a house a few yards down the street from his café. 'That was his house,' he said, 'I'm afraid I must leave you now as I have another customer.'

They thanked him for his help, gave him a fat tip and were left standing outside Jerome's house which, they both agreed later, was not remarkable in any way.

Lucy nudged him, 'Look!' she said motioning sideways. He turned his head to look at the building almost next door. The first thing that caught his attention was the beak gable and sitting above that the statue of a swan. There were four statues clinging to the front of the white house just above the level of the first floor.

'That's it!' she said excitedly,' Zwanenbroederhuis, or the Swan Brethren house; this is what we're looking for.'

The rain was becoming more persistent so they decided see if they could go inside there and then. They were met just inside the door by what they assumed was the curator of the building. Lucy explained that they were gathering information for a thesis on the life of Hieronymus Bosch and at first he looked doubtful, stating that at this time of the year they were not open to the public as a museum. Lucy explained that they had come from England to especially see the museum and he agreed to give them limited access to the exhibits. However, he soon warmed to the opportunity for airing his knowledge.

'Of course this building is often visited by the Dutch Royal Family,' he began pompously. 'Although Hieronymus Bosch was a member of this exclusive club, there are virtually no artefacts in our small collection which would be helpful with your project,' he said, his attitude suggesting the end of the conversation.

Lucy persisted, 'We've come all this way especially to see it; may we have a look around anyway?'

'I'm afraid . . . ,' he inclined his head, but before he could say anything else the man in the duffel coat appeared in the hallway. 'Excuse me,' said the curator and moved across to speak with him. There was a short conversation in Dutch, during which the two turned away from Jack and Lucy, the man in the duffel coat appearing to show something to the curator.

'How are we going to get in?' whispered Jack despairingly. 'Do you suppose we could just barge in anyway, get what we want and do a runner?'

'Not a chance,' she said, 'we don't even really know what we're looking for yet, so it's most unlikely we would spot it quickly enough before we were caught. No, I'm afraid we're just going to have to talk our way in, and out, somehow.'

As she said this they realised that the man in the duffel coat had disappeared and the curator was approaching them. 'You may look around freely he said, but first I must have your names and addresses.' This they duly did and the curator at last seemed satisfied. It occurred to Jack that this change of heart could be linked with the man in the duffel coat. He remembered seeing the man in the café; *are we being followed?* Before he could continue his train of thought the curator was motioning to them to proceed up a short flight of stairs. A telephone rang somewhere in the building and they were left alone as he went to answer it.

'I don't understand,' whispered Lucy, 'what happened there?'

'I don't know,' said Jack, 'but I think we're being followed, I'll tell you later.'

As they moved around the first floor Lucy commented on the closed circuit TV cameras positioned in one corner of each room. 'Have to be careful,' she mouthed, 'he can see everything we're doing.' They were beginning to despair, when finally they found what they were looking for. Lucy, nearly whooped with elation, then realised the Bible was locked in a display cabinet, with a camera trained directly on it.

Jack groaned; 'What now?' he said despairingly.

'Quick! Outside the room,' said Lucy and she motioned him outside the door. She pulled the laptop out of her hold all, switched it on and began to type instructions rapidly. To Jack's amazement the display cabinet suddenly appeared on the screen.

'That's what the camera's seeing. All I have to do now is freeze the camera's view and then it won't see us at all.'

she whispered. She typed in more instructions then told him to stand by the display cabinet. She was satisfied to see that Jack's image did not show on the camera.

'Look after the computer,' she said, and hurried into the room pulling a hairgrip out of her hair as she went.

'What are you going to do?'

'This!' she said triumphantly as she manipulated the hairgrip in the lock of the display cabinet and it obligingly sprang open.

Jack let out a gasp of admiration, 'Where did you learn how to do that?'

'Never mind that now, come over here and help me.'

Together they carefully lifted the bible from its case and began to flick through the yellowing pages as quickly as their age and condition would allow. Suddenly there was a movement from downstairs and they could clearly hear someone ascending from the floor below. Jack picked up the heavy book by its spine so that its pages hung down and muttered, 'Desperate measures.' A manila envelope fluttered to the floor. Lucy retrieved the envelope while Jack replaced the book and smartly moving to the door, picked up the computer and rammed it into the hold all in one swift movement. Lucy re-locked the cabinet just as the curator entered the room.

'Did you find what you were looking for?' he said with an oily smile.

'Oh! I think we may have,' replied Lucy.

'Ah! I see you have found the bible, the only thing here which may be of interest to you. It was presented by Hieronymus Bosch to his wife as a wedding gift.' As he said this he produced a small key and unlocked the cabinet. Jack and Lucy held their breath. The curator opened the cover of the book to reveal an inscription on the flyleaf which he translated and read aloud for them, 'The world is a haystack; everyone takes what he can.'

'What a strange thing to say to your new wife,' said Lucy.

'It's an old Dutch proverb denouncing materialism,' explained the curator.

'So he couldn't resist morally lecturing his wife on their wedding day,' cut in Jack, wishing he would just lock the book away.

The curator snapped the book closed and placed it back in the cabinet with the peevish comment, 'In those days the Church set strict moral codes. Of course it would appear strange in today's relaxed climate.'

A few minutes later, Jack heaved a sigh of relief as they stepped outside the building, 'Phew! That was close. You were brilliant picking the lock like that; let's go find a bank to rob.'

'You weren't so bad yourself; now we'd better check the booty,' she said, pulling the envelope from her hold all. Gingerly she levered open the fragile flap and peered inside. They could clearly see a few fine, red hairs tightly curled inside, secured with a small faded pink ribbon.

'Yes!' exclaimed Jack involuntarily.

'Calm down Jack, this is a just a means to an end and we don't know what end Jerome has in mind yet.'

'What now?'

'We go back to The Hague.'

'Why The Hague?' cried the astonished Jack.

'We're going to see my mother.'

'But I need to get home,' he protested.

'No problem, we'll catch the first flight in the morning, you'll be back home by the afternoon.'

CHAPTER 20

Carla and Albert had only just walked into the flat when the intercom buzzer sounded. Carla dropped her shopping on the kitchen table and went to answer the call.

Albert's six foot six, lean frame sagged into his favourite chair. His tanned face, kindly blue eyes and blond curly hair gave him a youthful appearance which belied his middle age. He reached for the evening newspaper, but as was his custom, closed his eyes after a few seconds and drifted off into a light nap.

'Mamma?' inquired the tinny voice.

Carla started in surprise, 'Lucia?'

'Si Mamma.'

'Lucia! Mia bambina! Avante pronto', she pressed the intercom button, releasing the door lock.

Lucy and Jack quickly made their way up to the flat where they were greeted enthusiastically by Carla.

'Comme.sta?' said Carla kissing Lucy on both cheeks while Jack looked on self consciously.

Lucy inclined her head towards him, 'English please Mama,' she whispered.

Carla's eyes twinkled mischievously as she looked Jack up and down. 'And who is this gorgeous hunk, my daughter has brought to see me?' she enthused.

Jack's face was by now, glowing red at this unwanted attention. Carla spread her hands towards him in welcoming fashion.

'English, no! He looks Italian, look at those deep brown romantic eyes, that handsome classical face and so slim and fit,' she said as she circled him seductively. 'Oh! No! My daughter, he must be Italian look at his delicious derriere.'

'Mama! Please!' she protested.

'He is your boyfriend, no?' interrupted Carla.

'No, he's just a good friend who's helping me out.'

'Mamma mia! How can this be? He is so handsome … very well … I shall have him for myself.'

Disturbed from his slumber by the excited chatter from the adjacent room, Albert unwound himself from his chair and swiftly came to Jack's rescue.

'Leave the poor lad alone Carla,' he said in a good-natured voice.

Carla's arms waved up and down, 'Spoila ma sport, Alberto, why you always spoila ma fun?'

'Not everybody understands your sense of humour darling,' he said, taking her by her slim waist and giving her an affectionate squeeze. She whimpered gently; he had temporarily tamed the lioness.

Lucy gave Albert an affectionate peck on the cheek, embraced her mother and formally introduced Jack, who had recovered from Carla's greeting and now had the opportunity to examine Lucy's mother at leisure. She was tall and elegant; Jack estimated about five foot eight inches, with black shoulder length hair. In spite of the fact that she must have been in her early forties, she only looked thirty, having a typical Italian beauty with large dark eyes and permanently pouting dark red lips. He looked closely at her face as she continued her animated conversation with Lucy. There were no discernable lines or other signs of advancing years. Apart from Lucy's Chinese eyes, the resemblance was striking. *This is probably where Lucy gets the impulsive side of her character*, he thought.

Albert glanced at Jack and noting his discomfort guided him to a chair in the adjacent room.

'Can I get you a drink?' he said, pouring himself a whisky at the discreet mini bar.

Jack's throat felt as if it was full of sawdust, 'Yes please, a coke would be nice.'

Albert smiled to himself as he poured the drink. 'What do you do Jack, I mean for a living?'

'Oh no!' said Jack quickly, 'I'm still at school.'

Albert handed him the coke, 'So what are you studying?'

'The sciences mainly, I'm hoping to have a career in science . . . .'

His voice faded away as he noticed a row of framed certificates on the wall which announced Albert's expertise and status as a scientific consultant to the oil industry.

'Oh Ja! Ja!' said Albert, following the line of his gaze, 'I have the small interest in this subject also, but that is my past, yours is the future,' and he raised his glass in a mock toast to Jack. 'A toast to the future; Lucy's a wonderful girl isn't she? How did you meet her?'

The question was slipped into the conversation with such ease Jack almost didn't notice the danger of supplying a truthful answer. He paused; desperately seeking a plausible response, one which he could be sure would fall in line with Lucy's explanation for the same question. Albert, noting his confusion, cut across his thoughts, 'You're not romantically connected then?'

'No! Lucy offered to help me with my thesis,' he blurted out. He immediately regretted his outburst, sensing he was getting deeper into a situation which could land Lucy in hot water.

'Is this why you come to Holland?' said the Dutchman.

If Albert had intended to interrogate me while Lucy's absent, he's certainly succeeding, thought Jack. Fortunately, he was rescued from further discomfort by Carla who burst into the room and flopped onto Albert's lap.

'Oh! Caro Alberto,' she purred, 'we must go out to dinner and celebrate.'

Albert smiled, 'Oh! Ja of course,' he agreed, reaching for his phone.

Jack felt out of place at dinner, dressed as he was in jeans, trainers and leather bomber jacket. His only previous experience of "going out to dinner" was when his parents had celebrated birthdays with him. He felt awkward and tongue tied, particularly in conversations with Albert, who was charming throughout, but quite intimidating.

Jack glanced around the restaurant, which was full of people in casual clothes enjoying each other's company. He began to relax. He decided he liked Holland. It was a country where the people seemed to have time for each other in a genuine laid back sort of way.

He was disturbed from his reverie by Lucy digging him in the ribs as she returned from the toilet and sat down beside him.

'Listen,' she said quietly, 'I've decided that the easiest way to get through this situation without causing problems for ourselves, is to admit that we are an item.'

Jack's mouth sagged open momentarily, 'But I've already told them we're not.'

'So have I, we'll just have to admit that we were telling a small porky. It will be easier this way, trust me.'

Jack's imagination began to conjure images of himself and Lucy as a couple. Sensing this, Lucy whispered, 'This is business, don't get the wrong idea.'

From that point onwards, Lucy took control of the dinner time conversation, occasionally turning to Jack, smiling sweetly, and including him in conversations in a caring sort of way. As they drank coffee it was clear to Jack that Lucy was preparing the way for the admission and neither Albert or Carla were surprised when she made it.

'My darling!' Carla exclaimed, 'We knew all the time that you were just been shy about it, and he's such a bella boy,' she concluded. Reaching across the table she put her hand against his face and flashed a flirtatious smile.

Jack shifted uncomfortably on his chair and felt his face begin to burn. This type of woman had only ever existed in his imagination before now. He was completely unable to cope with the attentions of Lucy's exotic mother.

Albert glanced at Lucy, 'Are you still involved in your father's work?'

'Oh yes,' she replied.

'How's it going?'

'We've come across some major problems,' she said guardedly.

Jack noted her reluctance to talk about it and quickly realised that if he knew the truth, Albert's role with a major oil company could result in some difficult family loyalties.

'I knew it would all come to nothing,' chimed Carla and raised her eyes heavenwards. 'All those wasted years,' she continued, 'for nothing.'

Later that evening Lucy and Jack were ushered into a spare bedroom by an exuberant Carla. Half a bottle of wine had removed any remaining constraints on her behaviour. 'Two beds I'm afraid,' she gushed waving an erratic hand at the small room, 'but I'm sure "amore" will find a way.' With a knowing wink she departed.

They flopped onto the beds and lay still for a while. Lucy began to chuckle and then laugh. Finally she was suffused with mirth. Jack propped himself up onto one elbow.

'What?' he said.

'Your face when Mama was making up to you, it was amazing,' she managed to splutter.

Jack pointedly turned with his back to her.

'Oh come on!' said Lucy, 'You were sweet.'

'Ugh!' was the strangled response from the other bed.

'You don't like my mama?'

'She's lovely,' said Jack and hesitated.

'But?'

'No buts, I was just thinking how like her you are.'

She became quiet. The silence seemed to stretch out for ever.

Finally he said, 'What's her relationship with Albert?'

'Oh! They've been together now for almost three years,' she replied, 'Mama met him shortly after the divorce, he's good for her.'

'What caused the divorce?'

'Work mainly, Father's work meant long periods away from home, so they just drifted apart and eventually agreed to call it a day.'

'What about you, how did it affect you?' enquired Jack.

'I was very much involved in Father's work, so I used to spend a lot of time with him. Mama got bored and got on with her career. I missed her terribly at first but in the end I suppose you get used to new circumstances and I was just pleased that she was happy.'

'You don't want Albert to know what you're up to, I mean with your work.'

'Absolutely not!' she replied, 'He's a very nice man and I think he and Mama are well suited, but there's no doubt where his loyalties would be if it came to taking sides. He is suspicious and obviously Mama has told him some of what she knows, which can't be very much but there's no point in telling him any more.'

For a long time Lucy was silent. He glanced over his shoulder. She was seated cross legged on the bed, completely motionless except for her shallow breathing. Her eyes were closed, her hands rested on her knees and her back was straight. Jack watched her as she meditated.

It had been a whirlwind of activity since the day she had interrupted his MP3 Player program on his way to school. He now had the opportunity to look at her more closely. Her jet black hair cascaded over her shoulders like a close fitting cloak spreading outwards down to her tiny waist. Her features were fine, unlike the usual oriental broad nose, hers was small and neat, and looked at in profile, was slightly turned up at the end. Her lips, full and red, were a European shape, pouting slightly, like Clara's. Her oval shaped face was signed off by a small determined chin, while her closed eyes, dark brown and almond shaped, required little make up to enhance their natural beauty. Jack allowed his gaze to linger over her slight figure, which unusually was revealed by a tight fitting top and skirt she had borrowed from her mother. She had tossed off her shabby trainers when she had fallen onto the bed to reveal exquisitely shaped pink feet.

Suddenly she opened one eye, 'You'll go blind,' she said.

'You *are* a witch,' returned Jack, 'you know what I'm thinking even when you're not in other dimensions.'

She smiled, 'No, this time it's because I'm a woman. But we have work to do,' she said, pulling the laptop from her hold all.

'You're not going to bring Jerome back to life here are you?' he said in alarm.

'No, I need to be sure we have computer back up just in case anything should go wrong, so I'll do that at home.'

'So what are you going to do?'

'Record and analyze the hair,' she replied.

'Aren't you forgetting something?'

'What?'

'You need the hair,' Jack spread his hands in a gesture of helplessness.

A look of horror crossed her face, 'What have I done with it?' she exclaimed in panic. She rummaged furiously in her hold all and finally gave a strangled cry, 'It's gone!'

'How careless,' said Jack calmly as he produced the envelope from his back pack, 'and I thought you knew everything?'

'You monster!' she howled and launched herself at him. Wrestling him to the floor she sat on his chest and pummelled his stomach with her small fists. Finally she tired and began to giggle. Jack felt the closeness of her and was aware of the strong smell of carbolic. *How could I ever have doubted her?* Meanwhile Lucy recovered her normal composure saying, 'Come on we have work to do, remember what's at stake here.'

She sat on the bed, the laptop computer in front of her and the lock of hair next to it. Crip had appeared when she switched on the computer and now presented a comical picture as he kept falling over on the soft bed. This was new terrain for him and he was plainly not programmed to cope. As she typed, she described what she was doing and why, Jack however, was tired and not really paying attention. Suddenly she stopped and turned to him as he yawned. 'You may need to know how to do this sometime in the future.'

'I doubt I could remember anything but the broad outline,' he protested, 'and I always have Crip to fall back on.'

At this Crip beamed his acknowledgement and in his enthusiasm fell off the bed and crashed onto the floor.

Realising she was pushing him too far, too early, and being anxious to avoid a confrontation, she quickly changed the subject, 'You said you thought we'd been followed?'

'I thought it was curious how that chap in the duffel coat appeared at the Swan place, it was almost as though he came to our rescue, just as things were beginning to get difficult. I'd love to know what he said to that curator chap, I'm sure he wouldn't otherwise have let us in.'

'What makes you think he was following us?' said Lucy.

'He was in the restaurant when we were having lunch. Do you suppose that Jerome is at the bottom of it, sending someone to keep an eye on us?'

'I doubt it, he doesn't need to do that, you can be sure he's watching us anyway. The only things he can produce in this dimension are those wretched demons.' She shuddered at the memory of them.

'Ugh! That's creepy,' he said, 'you mean he's watching our every move?'

'Well, wouldn't you if your future was on the line and you had nothing better to do?'

'I suppose so,' he said, 'it's a bit inhibiting though, don't you think?'

She didn't respond, but secretly agreed.

'How long will it take?' said Jack.

'You might as well get some sleep, this could be very lengthy,' she said sympathetically.

Try as he might he could not sleep. The steady clack of computer keys a constant reminder of the seriousness of Lucy's task. Several times he raised himself onto one elbow and peered at her in the light of the solitary bedside lamp. Her concentration was total, her dedication solid. In the early hours of the morning she finally gave a sigh and pushed the computer away from her. Crip, who had been sitting on the edge of it, promptly fell off and once more clattered onto the bare floorboards. She switched off the computer and he disappeared.

Jack, disturbed by the sudden noise, glanced across at her. She had resumed her position of meditation and was breathing steadily and deeply. When he awoke in the morning she was in exactly the same position. 'Didn't you sleep at all?' he said, astonished.

'I don't need to,' she replied, 'I meditate instead.'

CHAPTER 21

THE JOURNEY BACK to Schipol was uneventful. Jack felt uneasy until the aircraft was on its way. Any delay could have had disastrous consequences for their plan.

'How long have we got?' he said with a concerned glance at his watch.

'About four hours to the deadline, we should just do it.'

'What does Albert do for a living?' enquired Jack.

'He works for Shell in The Hague. He's a senior engineer on their exploration staff and goes out prospecting for new oilfields.'

Somehow Jack couldn't visualise Albert as a hard bitten oil prospector. At breakfast he had made a laddish remark about Jack's appearance, which bore the signs of little sleep. Jack did not protest, but allowed him to draw his own conclusions as to its cause. Lucy had simply smiled. Carla had fussed around them both wishing the next time they came they would stay longer. She was everything Jack's homely mum was not and in spite of her outrageous flirting, he had taken to her in a big way.

His eyes closed for a moment as he rested his head against the aircraft seat and he drifted into a half sleep state. The plane gave a jolt which shook him awake. 'We're approaching Heathrow, wake up lazybones. You slept on the train back to Amsterdam, fine company you were,' she said sarcastically.

Jack grunted, 'Is there much left to do?'

'Not really, we should just make it in time.'

After the routine landing the passengers disembarked and waited in the queue for passport control. As Lucy handed over her passport, the official gestured at two dark suited men standing nearby. Lucy looked at Jack apprehensively as they approached.

'Here take this,' she whispered urgently thrusting her hold all into his hand.

'Wha . . . ,why?' stammered Jack.

'Never mind, just take it,' she said, and the urgency in her voice awoke Jack from his drowsy state.

One man clamped a big hand around her upper arm saying, 'Would you like to come with us miss?' The thought of fleeing disappeared from her mind; she would have to talk her way out of this.

'Who are you?' she demanded.

'Police Miss' said the other man, fishing out his identity card.

'I have an urgent appointment,' she protested.

'This won't take very long Miss,' he said, steering her towards a door marked "Private".

Jack made to follow but the other man blocked his way saying, 'You're free to go lad.'

'But you don't understand,' blurted out Jack, 'we have to make our appointment, it's a matter of life and death.'

'You can wait if you like,' said the policeman, 'It shouldn't take too long.'

Lucy was bundled through the doorway and out of sight leaving Jack outside, frustrated and desperate.

. . . .

Livingstone walked into the office as Collins put the phone down.

'They've got her boss, holding her in an interview room,' he said.

'What about the lad?'

'They let him go.'

'Well I suppose we aren't really interested in him anyway, come on let's go,' he said rubbing his hands expectantly. 'Now at last we may find out what's going on.'

'What are we going to charge her with?' asked Collins, 'Faking her own death then causing her body to disappear while in police custody?'

'I don't know that we're going to charge her at all. I just want to get to the bottom of this so that I can sleep at night. We may keep her in custody overnight then dispatch her back to China, where she belongs,' he added.

. . . .

Jack looked around; he was surprised how cool he felt under the circumstances. It was as though he had been taken over by a different personality who was now directing his actions. *No time to think about that now*, he thought to himself as he slipped into the nearest toilets. He quickly occupied a vacant cubicle and sat down, closing the door behind him.

'Now to put my training into practice,' he muttered to himself. Setting the laptop computer on his knees, he inserted the DVD and loaded Lucy's quantum code. He was rewarded by the machine accepting her identification.

He selected the quantum entanglement facility, whereupon Crip appeared in the lid of the computer and slid down to the hinge falling in a heap at the bottom.

'You wan herp Jack?' he said.

Jack put a finger to his lips, 'Shush!'

Crip eyed him dispassionately and pointed at the screen where the words then appeared, 'I herp you get Rucie out'.

Jack looked at the spelling in disbelief, and then dismissed his unspoken criticism.

'OK.' he typed.

Crip looked pleased but Jack didn't entirely share his enthusiasm; the memory of the football match was still lingering in his mind.

He impatiently drummed his fingers on the keyboard as the machine searched for Lucy. The inside of the interview room appeared on the screen, much to Jack's relief, as viewed from above and towards one of the corners. Guided by Crip, Jack found that by moving the direction keys he could alter his field of vision around the room, *just like a video game,* he thought. He could clearly see Lucy sitting on a chair with her back against a wall adjacent to a door marked "Toilet". Scanning around he could see a female police officer seated at a table facing Lucy, scribbling furiously with her head bowed to her task. There was no one else in the room. Jack guessed that the door had been locked from the outside otherwise Lucy would probably have made a run for it. On the other side of the room from Lucy's position there was a computer on a table which could be seen from where they were both seated.

Mm, I'll have to take a chance that she doesn't look up from her writing, he thought to himself. Keeping one eye on the policewoman and one on his keyboard he zoomed in on the computer screen and typed a message, 'Go to the toilet! Jack.' Lucy, who had been shuffling her feet anxiously, stopped abruptly as she saw the message. Jack quickly deleted it before the policewoman looked up from her work. Lucy stood up and made the request. The policewoman motioned her to the toilet door then continued writing. Jack followed Lucy with the direction keys. Once she was inside, he energised the portal. Lucy stepped into it and promptly vanished. He de-energised the portal to the accompaniment of whooping and cheering from Crip. He scanned the interview room to ensure the policewoman was not aware the bird had flown and when satisfied switched off the laptop, placed it back in the hold all and flushed the toilet. As he emerged from the cubicle he froze in horror. One of the policemen was standing at the washbasins drying his hands.

The policeman looked him up and down sternly, 'I've had no instructions to detain you,' he began, 'but if you cause a disturbance in a public place by playing video games, I could change that.'

Jack decided to play along with the policeman's misunderstanding of Crip's exclamations and apologized. Relieved, he exited the toilets and headed for the train to London. Only when seated on the train did he realise he was shaking.

. . . .

Livingstone purposefully marched down the corridor to the interview room with a plain clothes policeman and Collins trailing behind. Collins had never seen him move this fast before. *It's remarkable,* he thought, as they strained to keep up with him, *how the impossible can be achieved when sufficiently motivated*.

Livingstone jangled the change in his pocket furiously, a sure sign of his impatience, and there was a gleam of victory in his eye as he waited for the plain clothes policeman to unlock the door. They entered the interview room to be greeted by the policewoman stretching and yawning as she stood up from her writing.

'Where is she then?' said Livingstone eagerly.

'She went to the toilet, but that must have been almost twenty minutes ago.'

'Get her out,' he demanded.

The policewoman emerged from the toilet, her face red with anxiety, 'I don't know how this can have happened sir because the doors have been locked and there's no other way out sir, but she appears to have disappeared sir,' she said meekly.

'Don't be silly,' said Livingstone trying to contain his impatience. 'Get a woman to do a man's job,' he muttered under his breath, as he barged past her and scanned the empty room. 'There's not even a window, she can't have escaped. She has to be in here somewhere,' he bawled.

He insisted they do a thorough search of the interview room although it was obvious to everyone else that she was not there. When he turned on the unfortunate policewoman with a barrage of expletives, Collins thought he was on the verge of a nervous breakdown and would have to be restrained. Recovering his composure he sat down at the desk, previously occupied by the policewoman, and began sketching the layout of the room, much to the amusement of the plain clothes officer. When he had satisfied himself that it was not possible to escape he turned on the plain clothes officer who was still wearing a half smile on his face.

'Wipe that stupid grin off your face! You've put her in a different room haven't you, to make me look stupid? Where have you put her?' he screamed, his nose barely two inches away from the unfortunate man's face.

The officer made to protest but Livingstone was not about to listen to any sensible attempt to resolve the mystery.

'Everybody out!' he yelled, 'I want the whole building searched as if you were looking for a rat, which, given the nature of this lady, you may well be!'

After an hour of fruitless searching, Collins persuaded Livingstone to give up and allow him to drive them back to headquarters. The senior policeman sat in the passenger seat muttering incoherently, occasionally waving his arms and gesticulating wildly.

After reporting to Smiley, he slouched back into the office, flopped down into his chair and looked dolefully at Collins, who avoided eye contact.

'I've been suspended for disobeying orders,' he said. There followed a long pause where his face became so contorted, Collins was afraid he was going to cry, or scream, or both. He didn't know which was preferable. 'I was only trying to find out what's going on; that's a policeman's duty isn't it?' he said despondently and let his head crash onto the desk.

. . . .

Lucy had observed all these happenings with unbridled amusement. She had never forgiven the authorities for labelling her father a spy and this represented some overdue revenge. She concluded that it would now be safe for her to operate from her house again as it was clear from what she had just witnessed that the police would no longer be interested in hounding her.

Jack arrived back at the house and reconstructed the portal. As he stood by the sparkling sphere in the conservatory, Lucy suddenly fell out of it on top of him, doubled up with laughter.

'Oh! That was fan . . . tas . . . tic,' she spluttered. 'I wish you could have seen them looking for me, it was better than "Keystone Cops", you were brilliant.' She threw her arms around his neck and kissed him on the cheek. Jack blushed at this sudden rush of affection. She held him at arms length and looked into his startled eyes, 'You're a real sweetie, I was right to choose you,' she said softly. She turned sharply on her heel and disappeared up to the computer room. Jack followed, his head spinning from her emotional outburst muttering, '"Keystone Cops"? I've never heard of it.'

'Now comes the really hard part,' she said, as they entered the computer room.

'You don't agree with doing this, do you?' he said.

'No, I can only see bad coming from it, but the alternative is even worse. There's absolutely no way we can stop him snatching Mandy again, and there's no point in going to the police, they simply wouldn't believe us. If only he didn't have the ability to produce those wretched demons, the worst he could do would be to give her nightmares and I'm sure he would quickly tire of that.'

'Trouble is, once you've re-created him in this dimension he can cause all sorts of mischief.'

'What I can't understand,' said Lucy thoughtfully, 'is that he must know, that given our knowledge of his D.N.A.

and quantum signature we can always put the genie back in the bottle at any time. That's what gives me the willies Jack, I don't understand his motives.'

'I suppose he reckons that all he has to do is to threaten someone else for us to cave in again.'

'I have this awful feeling that there's more to this than we know, that we're missing something which is right in our faces. It may be so obvious that we can't see it and we're unlikely to find out what it is until we've given him his freedom,' said Lucy.

She downloaded information from the laptop into the main computer and generated the portal with her quantum fingerprint. Jack took over at the computer as she made to go down to the conservatory, then, impulsively stopped her, and kissed her on the cheek with a whispered, 'Good luck, take care.'

Lucy stepped into the portal. Although her preparations had gone well, she was particularly nervous on this occasion believing that she may be transgressing the laws of nature by bringing a five hundred year old man back to life. She waited patiently for Jerome to appear as she knew he would. The first indication was a low hollow laugh, and then he was with her.

The message entered her consciousness, 'You have done well, and saved the child . . . for the time being. Now we can proceed.'

'What are you going to do with your new life?' she asked innocently.

Jerome paused in astonishment, 'Why! I shall continue the work I began five hundred years ago. The world has grown yet more sinful. There is much that requires my services.'

Lucy was determined to discover all she could before complying with his wishes in order to satisfy her nagging doubts regarding his motivation.

'You see yourself as the saviour of mankind, a sort of second Jesus?'

'No! That would indeed be blasphemy. We must each do what we can in accordance with our resources. You have done your part and should feel no responsibility for the result of your actions.'

'Unfortunately Jerome, my beliefs teach responsibility for actions always lie with the individual, unlike yours.'

'You aspire to be as great as God himself? The Renaissance gave you this self indulgent fantasy; repent sister and bow down before the real God lest you be sentenced to eternal damnation.'

'Like you were?' she snapped back; 'What *did* you do to deserve your fate? Oh! And by the way if it weren't for the Renaissance, you wouldn't have the possibility of another life.'

There was a lengthy silence as Jerome digested this latest swipe at his beliefs. 'All this idle chatter is getting us nowhere; get on with it,' he remarked testily.

'And if I refuse?'

'You would be very foolish to do so, I can abduct any child at will and your police can do nothing. My little friends can appear out of nowhere and do my bidding as you have already witnessed,' he reminded her.

'And you regard these as actions of a true Christian, murdering little children?'

'Life and death is also a natural law and so I would merely be acting as an agent to put that law into action.'

This bizarre self justification convinced her that further discussion was unlikely to reveal any more information about his intentions or deflect him from his purpose. She could foresee a continuing cycle of events where Jerome accumulated more and more power, free from the fear of his own death, always aware that he could be regenerated through threats of violence against innocents. What was morally correct was clear in her mind, but she could not bring herself to refuse his request and place other innocents at risk in the process. What she had in reserve was the ability to consign him back to oblivion, thereby curtailing his power. He must be aware of that and yet . . . what was his intention? This cat and mouse game still didn't make sense. Finally making her decision, she appeared on the computer screen.

'We have to do what he wants Jack,' she said and began to relay instructions. Jack distinctly heard Jerome's triumphant chuckle and shivered. Were they releasing an evil entity on an unsuspecting world? One thing for sure thought Jack, we may be able to return him to his penance but we'll never be able to kill his intentions and he's always likely to pop up again somewhere else. Another thought occurred to him as he busied himself typing in Lucy's instructions, wasn't that also true of the Devil? Having witnessed the events of the past few days he did not doubt, that the Devil could exist and cause mayhem at every opportunity. He carefully followed Lucy's instructions for marrying together D.N.A. and quantum signature through quantum entanglement. Body and consciousness were to be re-introduced to each other after five hundred years of separation.

Lucy's voice cut through his thoughts, 'He wants you to go down to the portal Jack, be careful.'

With acute misgivings he made his way down to the portal and awaited there the result of their efforts.

The sphere was glowing brilliant blue and turquoise intermittently, Jack stood in front of it, beads of cold sweat standing out on his forehead and his nerves tingling in anticipation.

Suddenly it turned bright orange and with an enormous belch spat three slimy demons onto the floor. Jack started back then turned to make a dash for the door but they were too quick for him. Two demons grabbed an arm each while the third wrapped itself around his legs. The stench from their vile bodies was awful causing Jack to retch. Struggling was futile against their combined strength. He watched as the portal pulsated, stretched vertically and the hooded, menacing figure of Jerome Van Aken stepped from it into the conservatory.

'Take him upstairs,' he hissed.

CHAPTER 22

DIPPER MADE HIS way to Jack's house with his peculiar shambling gait, a consequence of him being born with one leg shorter than the other.

He stepped back smartly as Betty Dawkins opened the door. 'Is Jack in, missus Dawkins?' he enquired.

Betty looked puzzled and then slightly worried.

'No! I thought he was with you; didn't he stay with you last night? He said he had some difficult homework. Mind I suppose he didn't say he was staying with you, we just assumed . . . .'

'Naw, he didn't stay with me,' said Dipper, 'don't worry, I'll ask around, and I'll let you know.'

He turned away from the doorstep, a suspicion forming in his mind that Jack had spent the night with Megan. He knew that challenging Megan would have little effect, but decided to give it a go anyway just to gauge her response.

Megan answered the door.

'What do you want?' she said curtly.

'I'm looking for Jack,' he said with a knowing smile.

'And why would you suppose he might be here, nerd brain?'

'Well, as nobody's seen him for two days, I assumed he was nesting with you.'

'Cheeky sod!' said Megan and then paused, a frown crossing her face, 'Isn't he at home, he should be back by now?'

'Back! Back from where?'

'Never you mind frog-face,' she said, biting her lip.

A voice boomed from inside the house, 'If you're looking for that Dawkins boy, he isn't here. He's nothing but trouble, I've told her not to see him anymore or she'll feel the weight of my hand.'

'Now Da,' said Megan, 'don't frighten poor Dipper, he doesn't know you wouldn't hurt a fly see.'

The hairy giant appeared in the doorway startling Dipper. 'Now *he* seems like a good dependable lad,' he boomed, peering at the increasingly apprehensive boy, 'you could do worse than him gal.'

She viewed Dipper as if he had just emerged from a dustbin. 'Oh come on Da,' replied Megan, 'he's nothing more than the school computer geek. I'd be the laughing stock of the whole school if I took up with him.'

Thoroughly intimidated, Dipper beat a hasty retreat.

This conversation troubled Megan. Jack should be back by now. Why hadn't he called her? She decided to go to Lucy's house and investigate.

. . . .

The demons scurried up the stairs dragging Jack with them. As she appeared out of the portal, Jerome grabbed Lucy by one arm and forced it around her back and up towards her head.

'Let go! You're breaking my arm,' she yelled.

'Now then,' he said, his foul breath wafting across her face, 'we don't want to attract any attention from the neighbours, do we?' He shook her violently whereupon she ceased to struggle.

'I was right the first time,' she muttered, 'you are a slime ball, and you smell like the Devil's armpit.'

'Be quiet, or I'll break your neck,' growled Jerome.

'What do you want from us, we've done what you wanted,' she snarled.

'My word, you are a little tigress aren't you?' Jerome mocked as he tightened his grip on her arm. 'Oh no! I haven't finished with you yet.'

'Ouch! You're hurting me,' wailed Lucy.

'Upstairs!' He ordered, pushing her roughly while still holding her bruised arm. As they made their way upstairs Jerome snatched a ceremonial two edged sword off the wall and brandished it briefly in his free hand.

'Oh yes!' he remarked, 'This will do nicely.'

The demons had been busy while they waited for their master and had tied Jack's hands behind his back with the curtain ties. He was in the opposite corner of the room to the computer, on his knees with his head bowed.

It was by now quite dark outside, the only light in the room coming from the computer itself. Jerome flung Lucy into the computer chair then went across to Jack and slid the blade of the sword under his chin.

'Now I think you can understand that any attempt to escape will result in your boyfriend's throat being cut,' he said in a matter of fact voice.

Lucy gave him a baleful look, 'What do you want?' she spat out.

'Patience my dear, after five hundred years I must enjoy my new existence for a while. I am rather interested in your little plaything,' he waved a hand at the computer. 'In my day much of what you have achieved here was done by alchemy and witchcraft, however I believe you have progressed much farther than that.' Lucy eyed him carefully watching for any weakness she could exploit, but said nothing.

'Come now, you weren't this shy a few minutes ago, cat got your tongue?' As he said this he grabbed Jack by the hair and pulled his head back, then made a cutting motion with the sword. Jack gave a yelp, 'Don't tell him anything Lucy,' he managed to squeeze out. Lucy looked away in disgust and horror. What was the brute after?

'Yes it's true you can do some impressive tricks with your quantum entanglement, as you call it. I have noted that you can convert matter to energy and energy to matter, however there is one thing which is in your power you have yet to attempt.' He paused and observed the effect of his statement on Lucy.

Lucy eyed him suspiciously, 'Yes?' she said.

'Yes, I am referring to your ability to destroy energy.'

Lucy gasped, 'How did you . . .' her voice tailed off as she realised what he was saying.

Jack lifted his head, 'What does he mean Lucy?' He received a kick in the ribs from one of the demons for his trouble and bent forward again panting heavily.

'Well?' demanded Jerome.

'It's not possible,' said Lucy, 'the laws of physics forbid it. If it were possible the results could be disastrous.'

'Educate me child,' said Jerome watching her closely.

'If it was possible to destroy energy it would result in a chain reaction. It may even change the planet or beyond. We just don't know what would happen. Why do you want to know? What do you intend to do?'

Jerome paused. Lucy sensed indecision. Had he realised the full implications of his query? She decided to press home the argument.

'If I were to destroy even a small amount of energy, it could cause an unstoppable disaster.'

Jerome looked puzzled for a moment, then the look of horror she had previously seen cross his face reappeared. The dark shadow spread from the edges of the cowl inwards. His face contorted in fear and rage, he screamed at her, 'You will do my bidding!'

'No I cannot,' she replied steadfastly, 'it could have terrible consequences.'

Once more he paused and Lucy had the impression that he was involved in a massive internal struggle. The shadow on his face became alternately lighter and darker. It was then she realised he was being manipulated like a grotesque marionette. Her determination to resist grew with this knowledge. She decided to take a chance, 'Show yourself whoever you are, you evil monster,' she said, defiantly.

From his position on the floor Jack began, 'Lucy, do you think that . . . ?'

'Quiet Jack!' she interrupted, 'There's more to this than we have seen so far.'

'You *will* destroy energy,' interjected Jerome.

'What energy?' she said with a horrified glance at Jack. Jerome followed her gaze, 'Oh no, not his . . . mine!'

Lucy was astounded, struggling to understand why he would want his energy and matter destroyed when he had just been given a new lease of life.

'I can see you are confused, let me explain. When I was alive, the last time that is, the population of Den Bosch acclaimed my paintings as the product of genius, until they became aware that the hidden messages were directed at them. They did not want to be told they were sinners and so, they declared me a heretic, me! A bastion of the Church, those lubbards had the nerve to call *me* heretic.' Jerome's face was contorted with the pain of the memory. 'I have no doubt,' he continued, 'that this life would be no different, possibly even worse.'

'So why do you want it?' ventured Lucy.

For a moment Jerome's face became sad, 'It is the only way.'

'I don't understand,' said Lucy, hoping to deflect him from his purpose.

'I could not endure the prospect of being confronted with myself for eternity. When I detected your activities I realised you could release me from purgatory by destroying both aspects of me, matter and energy. In order to ensure your compliance I had to become material in this world so that you could do this, for I know you cannot create or destroy in other dimensions.'

'So that's it,' said Lucy softly. 'What did you do wrong to find yourself in purgatory?'

'I am no more a sinner than you are,' said Jerome his voice becoming agitated and his eyes flashing. 'It was undeserved, but now I am going to escape and in the process I will prove to you, that even you, with all your fine morals and religion can be vilified as was I, through no fault of your own.'

'You can release yourself from purgatory,' said Lucy desperately, 'there is another way. Someone, or something, is misleading you in order to destroy this world. You can repent and become clean once more, but first you have to put aside your ego and admit that you were wrong . . . but I can't do what you ask, it's not possible.'

Jerome suddenly bounded across the room and whirled the sword around his head. With one swipe he cleaved the statue of the Buddha in two, then leaning across the filing cabinet snarled in Lucy's face, 'If you do not, your boyfriend dies.'

She gulped back the tears as her resolve began to wane, there was no way out, she would have to do his bidding. It was clear that Jerome had nothing to lose and he was going to see this through to the bitter end, turning her into a sinner in the process. She steeled herself and began to type the algorithms. Suddenly she stopped with her fingers poised above the keyboard, 'I can't do it,' she wept. 'I can't kill anyone, not even you. You'll have to do it yourself, it's all set up, all you have to do is press the "enter" key, please don't make me do it,' she begged.

Jerome scowled, 'Oh no! That would not do at all. This *must* be your responsibility. For all your sweet innocence, you are just as capable of sin as I, and it is my last wish that I prove it,' he thundered. Every word shook Lucy's nerves until she was trembling uncontrollably, tears streaming down her face.

The blade flashed again without warning in the light of the computer screen and Jack gave a howl of pain as two of his fingers were lopped off as though pruning a branch. He wrestled with the bonds, but to no avail.

'Do it!' demanded Jerome, 'Unless you want to see your boyfriend disappear, piece by piece.'

Lucy's finger hovered, shaking violently, over the keyboard, 'I can't! I can't!' she screamed.

Jerome rose to his full height with the sword above his head and brought it down in a flashing arc with all his weight on the back of Jack's unprotected neck. His head wobbled for a fraction of a second the eyes bulging grotesquely. Blood welled around the cut. The head fell forward onto the floor with a dull thud, followed by a fountain of blood pumping from the hole between his shoulders. The head rolled across the floor, eyes darting back and forth, lips quivering. Lucy screamed, lurched forward and fell across the keyboard in a dead faint.

Another scream had echoed Lucy's. Megan had burst into the room and seeing the carnage acted instinctively.

'You vile bastard!' she screamed and launched herself at the surprised Jerome, wrestling him to the floor. Her hands clamped around his neck, and shook his head back and forth like a rag doll. Jerome's eyes were beginning to bulge, when the demons retaliated and jumped onto her back. Jerome gave a tremendous heave and threw Megan off him. She staggered back and slipping in Jack's blood fell to the floor. The demons snarled and seeing her recumbent body leaped on her once more. Jerome rose above Megan, sword in hand preparing to strike.

'Rucie! Rucie! Wake up!' shouted Crip in Lucy's ear. She groaned, slipped sideways and fell to the floor.

Crip jumped onto the keyboard and stamped on the "enter" key. For a moment there was complete calm, everything frozen as in a tableau; then a curious orange halo enveloped Jerome as he became statue like, the sword suspended above his head. Megan was the first to move, seizing her chance she yanked at Jerome's leg which promptly folded under him, sending him crashing to the floor. The sword spun across the floor as Jerome's already decomposing body crumpled. A hollow laugh echoed around the room, 'I win, I win!' she heard vaguely as she pounded the empty cloak.

In the early winter gathering dusk, the ground began to grind and shake as in an earthquake. A ghostly figure flitted across the garden of number fourteen, making its way towards the conservatory. Simultaneously a portly man stepped out of the still glowing sphere in the conservatory. They conversed briefly then made their way up the shuddering staircase to the computer room while the shaking began to gather momentum. The computer room door was hanging drunkenly from one hinge; pieces of plaster were dropping from the ceiling onto the unconscious figure of Lucy and Jack's corpse. Megan was sprawled on the floor at the side of Jack's body wailing uncontrollably and did not see the newcomers enter. Of Jerome and his demons, there was no sign. The portly man lifted Lucy into a sitting position against the filing cabinet, sat down and began to type furiously, while the other went to the assistance of Megan.

The floor gave a tremendous heave as he helped her to her feet, 'Come on Megan let's get you out of here,' he shouted over the roar of the howling wind which was gradually building to gale like proportions. She turned her tear stained face towards him, 'It's you!' she said in astonishment, 'What are you doing here?'

'Never mind that now,' said Chalky, 'let's get you outside before the whole building collapses.' He put his arm around her and they both swayed precariously out of the damaged door.

The room was rocked periodically by tremors which were getting worse. Lucy began to stir. She looked up at the man sitting at the computer, 'Father!' she gasped.

'Get out Lucy! Before it's too late,' he shouted.

Lucy scrambled to her feet as she realised what her father was attempting.

'How can I help?' she yelled.

'Put Buddha back together, and then get out.'

She did as she was bidden and hastily retreated into the garden. On finding Megan standing with Chalky she flung her arms around her and tried to console her as they wept hysterically from the shock of Jack's demise.

'Stay here!' ordered Chalky and went back into the house to assist Lucy's father.

As he re-entered the computer room, Chalky could see a faint blue glow encircling the statue of the Buddha. He watched the glow intensify and simultaneously the earth tremors and wind decreased in their ferocity.

'What are you doing?'

'Putting him in prison,' said Chu.

'You're converting him to matter?'

'Consciousness, spirit, ego, everything just matter, here!' and he pointed to the Buddha, 'Where we can keep . . . ha . . . eye on him.'

There was a sudden bright flash followed by a faint strangled cry. The two halves of the Buddha welded themselves together and the earthquake ceased abruptly.

'Got him!' yelled Chalky triumphantly, 'Now let's see what we can do for the poor unfortunate lad here.'

Lucy and Megan's terror subsided with the easing of the earthquake and the howling wind. Cold and miserable, they clung to each other in the garden until they thought it safe to venture indoors. Choking back their tears, they made their way through the conservatory, past the dimly glowing portal and into the kitchen. Little was said as they sat at the kitchen table, drained of emotion and exhausted, still shaking from the horror of what they had just witnessed.

Lucy surveyed Megan's appearance. She was covered in Jack's drying blood, while wounds inflicted by the demons were bleeding freely. Her clothes were ripped and torn where the demons had held her with their sharp claws.

'God you look frightful,' she said. 'That man with my father is that your teacher?'

'Yes that's Chalky White,' she said, through bitter tears. 'How did your father get here?'

'Through the portal; but why is Chalky White here?'

'I don't know; I can't think straight at the moment. I remember he took over as physics master shortly after all this started,' she waved a tired hand vaguely in the direction of the conservatory.

'Someone's going to have to tell Jack's parents what happened,' said Lucy, her voice trembling. Tears began welling in their eyes as the awful realisation became apparent and they hugged each other once more for comfort.

Footsteps echoed down the stairs and Chalky, attracted by the light in the kitchen, came in. 'How are you girls? You've been through an awful experience tonight, you must both be exhausted. Don't worry, everything will soon be back to normal,' he said cheerfully.

Lucy and Megan stared at him incredulously as he pulled out a mobile phone and dialled a number, as though he was ordering a pizza.

'Evening,' said Chalky into the phone, 'yes its White here, can you make sure that any reports of disturbances at fourteen Lichfield Avenue are accepted but not acted upon. I don't want "Sasquatch" interfering this time.'

Lucy's curiosity was aroused, 'Who's "Sasquatch"?'

'Just a very inquisitive and persistent Detective Inspector,' said Chalky, with a meaningful glance at her.

'Are you a policeman?' asked Lucy.

'Sort of, I'll tell you all about it later. Right now there is someone I want you both to meet.'

'What about Jack?' demanded Megan, 'Haven't you noticed he's dead, you heartless sod?'

'Hey, look!' said Lucy pointing at Megan, 'Your clothes; all the blood's gone!' Megan looked down in astonishment. Jack's blood had completely disappeared, leaving only the fresh blood oozing from her wounds.

'Yes! Of course, that's why I want you to meet someone,' said Chalky with a wink. 'Come with me!'

Still shivering, the distraught girls followed him through to the conservatory and sat huddled in cane chairs, miserably waiting in the semi-darkness lit by the portal.

Suddenly the portal intensified and expanded. A figure was just discernable within the blue semi-opaque light. It approached with a mechanical gait, stepped into the conservatory and then stood motionless, staring straight ahead. Lucy and Megan gasped.

'My God it's Jack,' cried Lucy and they both rushed forward to embrace him.

'I am not programmed for human emotions!' said the figure in a hollow monotone, eyes staring straight ahead. He held out his arms in front of him, ready to push them away. Lucy and Megan halted in confusion.

'What have you done to him?' cried Megan.

Chalky shifted uncomfortably, a startled expression on his face. 'Well it seemed like a good opportunity to try out a few experimental things we had been working on, however . . . ' his voice tailed off.

The girls turned on him as one, 'How could you?' spluttered Megan.

Chalky spread his hands in an expression of submission. 'Well at least he's alive . . . sort of.'

Megan sank back into the chair, curled into a tight ball and began to weep, while Lucy prowled around the motionless figure. Finally she prodded him in the stomach. A faint smile trembled at the corners of his mouth while his expressionless eyes showed no sign of emotion. Gathering a ball of spittle in her mouth she looked up at his face her tear stained eyes dancing with mischievous excitement and her cheeks puffed out. Jack, sensing what was about to happen ducked and fell laughing on the floor. Lucy fell on him, tickling him until he could barely breathe from laughing.

'You sod!' cried Megan, leaping from the chair and joining in the fray.

Finally, all three lay panting on the floor from their exertions while Chalky looked on and beamed in satisfaction.

'Well perhaps we got it right after all,' he said.

CHAPTER 23

CHU OCCUPIED THE one seat in the computer room as he meticulously filed and backed up the programs which had hurriedly been thrown together to dismiss Jerome and convert his energy before it was completely destroyed. The teenagers sat cross-legged in a semi circle on the bare floorboards. All that remained to suggest the drama of the past hour was the crumpled cloak, the ceremonial sword and the noxious smell. All evidence of Jack's execution had disappeared with his reconstitution.

Lucy was intrigued, 'What did you do to him, Father?' she asked, pointing at the cloak.

Chu stood up and picked up the heavy statue of the Buddha in both hands, 'Here! See, here,' he said, turning the statue around. On the back of the idol could be distinctly seen the outline of a lion's head.

'I don't remember seeing that before,' said Lucy.

'No! You wouldn't, daughter; that is family symbol of Jerome. I . . . ha . . . convert energy to mass and capture him in here. Symbol then appeared.'

'You mean he's stuck in there forever?' Megan shuddered, 'How awful.'

'He . . . ha . . . has no consciousness, he's not aware of his condition,' said Chu.

'It couldn't happen to a nicer chap,' said Jack feeling his neck gingerly.

'So what about Jack?' said Lucy.

'As good as new,' said Jack enthusiastically.

'He's better than that,' chipped in Chalky.

Jack looked confused, 'What do you mean?'

'Well, what I said about trying out some experimental things is true. For some time now we have been ready to try implanting the facility for quantum entanglement in the brain. A large portion of a normal brain is hardly ever used, so we decided to use and program it with what you might call a sixth sense, or extra sensory perception. ESP for short, you may have heard of it.'

As he saw some doubt cross Jack's face, Chu cut in quickly, 'Jack is first person to receive wonderful gift which give him special powers. He will do quantum entanglement in head, not on computer.'

Lucy gave an appreciative whistle, 'I could do with that myself,' she said.

'When Jack has proved usefulness, you shall have,' agreed her father.

Jack still looked troubled, 'Do you have a problem with that?' asked Chalky.

'It's not so much that,' replied Jack, 'it's the whole thing really, I mean, what we're discussing here is top secret I expect?'

Chalky nodded.

'And I suppose you represent some shadowy organisation within the British Government?'

Chalky nodded again.

Jack smiled, 'And you don't want me to ask any more questions about it?'

Chalky smiled in return, 'I see your new powers are working already.'

'My problem is, I'm only seventeen, as is Megan, but without any choice, we are part of a secret which we will have to carry for the rest of our lives.'

'I can see your problem,' said Chalky, 'you think your whole life will now be controlled by the department I represent.'

'Yes, that's it.'

'It's not really a problem for you, or us. Obviously you'll have to sign the Official Secrets Act, but that's no more than any recruit in the army would have to do. You will continue to lead a normal life in whatever way you choose, however, should you decide to become an operative, we would call on your special skills from time to time. All we ask for the moment is that you make a choice.'

'Does this apply to me?' asked Megan.

'Yes of course,' said Chalky, 'you would be quite useful to us, as you obviously already have psychic tendencies, probably something to do with your Druidic background.' he laughed.

Megan sniffed scornfully, 'I suppose you've been spying on Jack and me for some time, so why didn't you stop this awful business earlier?

'You're right,' agreed Chalky, 'it was a risky strategy, but we had to follow through with it to understand what was going on. Rest assured we always knew we could step in and stop the whole thing.'

'Strategy!' echoed Megan, 'Some strategy that almost brought the world to an end. And you think I should sign up to your cowboy organisation for life? Dream on boyo, I think you ought to stop all this before it's too late and you destroy the planet.'

'I'm afraid that cannot be done,' said Chalky slowly. 'In the first place there was never any possibility of the planet being destroyed. The effect was always going to be self limiting and localised. Jerome, and more importantly whatever was controlling him, was not aware of that when they tried to make their mischief. Secondly I'm afraid we are now your best option. Sooner or later science in other countries will tread the same path as us. Those countries may be hostile and threatening. We can't afford to risk that, we have to stay ahead of the game or risk possible slavery at best or, at worst . . . annihilation.'

Megan looked heavenwards, despair on her face, 'So we're caught in a trap, all of us?'

'I wouldn't say it's a trap, we just have to make the best of it,' said Chalky sympathetically. 'At least we're not as caught as our friend here,' he said reflectively turning the statue of the Buddha around in his hands.

'However, there is a way out if you *really* want it; but it involves erasing some of your memory.'

Chalky glanced at Chu and receiving an acquiescent nod continued to explain how it could be done.

'It's not without risk,' he continued 'I want you to think about it over the next few days and tell me what you want to do.'

'Risk?' said Megan, 'You mean if I went for that option I could end up a vegetable?'

'Leeks can be attractive,' said Jack flippantly.

Megan gave him a frosty stare, 'And to think I'm in this mess because of you. I've fought demons and witches, been frightened out of my wits not to mention watching you die.' Tears were streaming down her face as she shouted,

'And now you want to spoil the rest of my life, I hate you, I hate all of you!' She ran out of the room crying hysterically.

Lucy was watching Jack intently. He turned to her, 'You think she'll be a liability don't you?'

Lucy gave a brief nod, 'I don't think there's any room for emotional involvement,' she said.

Chalky found her in the bathroom sitting on the toilet seat, sobbing as she dabbed antiseptic on her bitten legs.

She looked up at him tearfully, 'I know I should be brave but . . . .'

'Now then, you have been exceptionally brave already,' said Chalky putting a comforting arm around her shoulders. 'We can always erase all memory of what has been happening to you. Anything that would prompt any memory would be removed.'

'What about Jack?'

'Particularly Jack,' he said, deliberately misunderstanding her question, 'from what I know of your relationship he would be like a lightening conductor for your memories.' He held her head against his chest and stroked her hair gently, 'We would have to make Jack appear to you like a different person . . . ,' he paused, 'someone like Dipper, perhaps.'

Megan went rigid under his touch, 'Oh no! Definitely not! I'm not going to have that,' she exploded, and jumping to her feet sent the bottle of antiseptic scudding across the bathroom floor. 'I'll do whatever you say, but not that!'

Chalky allowed himself a sly smile and took her hand, 'Come then, let's tell the rest of the team.'

Lucy glanced nervously first at her father and then at Chalky, who gave her a reassuring nod, as he entered the computer room with the calmer Megan.

'Megan has agreed to join us,' he said.

Megan turned to Lucy, 'I know what you're thinking,' she said, 'it's written all over your face, but you're wrong.' She looked directly at Jack, 'I will not let anybody down,' she said emphatically.

Chalky, picked up on this, 'Megan, I think with our help, you could be trained very easily to decipher the wave patterns of people's brains and read their minds. How would you feel about that?'

'Now that could be very useful,' she said, glaring at Lucy.

'What about you Jack, are you with us?' said Chalky.

'What if I decide to spill the beans?' he said.

'No one in authority would believe a seventeen year old boy with such a wild story, would they Jack?'

'I suppose not,' he agreed, 'can I give it some thought for a few days?'

'Yes, of course.'

Lucy turned to Jack anxiously, 'You were right about the possibility of invasion from other dimensions, it could happen again, anytime, anywhere, and if it does we shall need someone who's experienced like you, to help us deal with it.'

Jack looked at Lucy curiously, 'How much did you know about the British Government's involvement in this?'

'Nothing!' she said, 'It would have made things a lot easier had I known.'

Jack nodded, 'That is for sure,' he said with feeling.

'Unfortunately,' said Chalky, 'we would not have learned a great deal if we had told you we were keeping an eye on you. In this way we discovered how to apply our knowledge and just as importantly we realised the quality of you three.'

'That chap in the duffel coat in Holland,' said Jack, 'was he one of yours?'

'Yes! He was, but enough of this, I think we should celebrate our success with a meal, as I'm sure you're all as hungry as me. Jack, Megan, better telephone your parents and tell them where you're going,' said Chalky, handing over his mobile, 'I don't want to lose my job at school by being irresponsible with the pupils,' he grinned.

Megan made to object, 'I can't go out in this state,' she cried, 'look at me! I've got tears in my clothes, I'm still bleeding and I smell of disinfectant and demons.'

'Darling,' crooned Lucy, 'you look as lovely as you ever did.'

'At least you kept your head' interjected Jack, fingering his neck.

'That is so typical of you Jack Dawkins, only ever thinking of yourself, so you do,' cried Megan.

'You two *should* be married,' remarked Lucy acidly.

Chalky intervened quickly, 'Now then team, you have to learn stop bickering or I may have to release my own personal demons among you! If you care to step into the portal Madam,' he said, turning to Megan, 'I think we can fix your wounds quite easily, as for your torn clothes . . . we cannot conjure up a seamstress; there is a limit to this technology which even we cannot overcome.'

They left for the restaurant in Chalky's car failing to notice a portly young man on the opposite side of the street. As they drove away he turned to go, and the glow of the street lights glinted briefly on his thick glasses as he limped away.

. . . .

Other diners gazed at them curiously as they entered and were shown to a table in a remote corner of the restaurant, carefully chosen by Chalky. 'We certainly add to the ambience,' he remarked, as the waiter screwed up his nose against the peculiar odour.

Later, after their meal, Jack had a whispered conversation with Lucy. 'How much do you know about my father's activities?' he said. She looked away as though trying to avoid the question.

'When I was in the other dimension and being put back together by your father,' persisted Jack, 'I found that by thinking of something or somewhere, I could be there and experience scenes as they were happening; as an observer.'

Lucy nodded tersely, hoping he wouldn't pursue the enquiry, 'Yes that's how it works.'

'So, I found myself thinking about my father and his reluctance to agree with my scientific career. It occurred to me that my parents had a humble lifestyle, considering Dad's status as a partner in a law firm. So either he wasn't been paid very much, or he was squandering most of it.'

Lucy nodded again.

'And guess what? I was suddenly witnessing a gambling club inhabited by prostitutes, lap dancers, pimps and . . . my father!'

Lucy's face was grim, her mouth compressed into a tight line. 'Yes?'

'You knew didn't you?'

Tears welled up in her eyes, 'I'm sorry Jack, I couldn't bring myself to tell you.'

'It's ironic isn't it, I've just being decapitated trying to prevent someone infesting the world with sin, only to find my own father in the Garden of Earthly Delights.'

'That's not all,' said Lucy miserably.

'What could be worse?'

'Your father is being blackmailed by Megan's father.'

Jack was momentarily stunned into silence.

'You mean my father is paying him to keep quiet about his other life?'

Lucy nodded.

'What can I do?'

'Not much, short of bottling him up in another statue.'

'But, he's my father Lucy! I *have* to do something about this.'

'Jack, I know this is hard for you, but you would be throwing your life away if you tried to intervene. You remember we talked about attractors being formed by the environment of a seascape?'

'Vaguely, oh yes! I remember, you said the sea has no way of learning when the environment changes.'

'Well people's habits are like attractors and are produced in response to their environment. I can't see your father's environment changing, can you?'

'But people can learn,' interrupted Jack.

'Yes of course they can but only if they want to. Your father enjoys his habit as Megan's father enjoys taking money from him. You can't force them to change if their habits are formed over many years. You saw how Jerome struggled to accept that he had to change to bring about his own salvation, and he'd had five hundred years to think about *his* mistakes.'

'I suppose so.'

'And anyway how are you going to convince Megan's father to stop extorting money from yours? It's obviously keeping him in comfort.'

'What about Megan, does she know?'

'Not yet, but she will, once she starts entering other dimensions.'

'What a mess,' shuddered Jack, 'Parents! Who'd have 'em. Maybe I could influence them through the other dimension as you did with Megan and Dipper.'

She shrugged, 'Well, it may be worth a try, but you'll have to get Megan to help you with that one.'

Jack was silent again; even with the special powers he had now inherited, there was no easy answer. He silently cursed the knowledge and new responsibilities they had brought with them.

Lucy leaned forward and kissed him tenderly on the cheek, then withdrew rapidly as she saw Megan watching them. 'I am truly sorry Jack, believe me I didn't know any of this before I asked you to help me.'

'That's OK, it's not your problem, never was, and you're right . . . it doesn't have to be mine. I think the sooner I get off to university the better, don't you?'

'Absolutely!' she said.

. . . .

Jack got home later in the evening to be faced with a thinly veiled inquisition from his parents.

'So you took Megan out for a meal?' said his mother, flushing with pleasure.

'Not exactly,' said Jack guardedly.

'What do you mean?' she said.

'Well, I suppose you could say I went Dutch, but not with Megan,' he replied, with a secretive grin.

'I don't understand these modern relationships,' chimed in his father predictably. 'In my day when we took a girl out for a meal, we didn't expect her to pay for it.'

Jack could feel himself cringing, it was as though the walls were slowly closing in on him, threatening to squeeze out his vital spark and consign him to a dull grey, tedious existence.

'How did your homework go with your friend?' asked his mother, changing the subject quickly.

Jack started, and then he remembered the excuse he had given them for not going home the previous evening. 'Oh, it was all right, I learned an awful lot, mostly about myself,' he added under his breath.

'Well whatever the subject,' said his father, 'the discipline of solving problems will stand you in good stead when you take up the law.'

Jack looked at the clock on the mantelpiece. It was ten minutes to ten. He thought of the many times he had stared at that clock with dismay, watching it measuring out his life. He concentrated on the hands and with an effort of will knotted them together. The clock stopped abruptly.

He had made his decision.